Stories by Contemporary Writers from Shanghai

T0192968

# THE EAGLEWOOD PAVILION

This book is edited and designed by the Editorial Committee of *Cultural China* series

Text by Ruan Haibiao
Translation by Wu Xiaozhen
Cover Image by Quanjing
Interior Design by Xue Wenqing
Cover Design by Wang Wei

Assistant Editor: Cao Yue
Copy Editor: Gretchen Zampogna
Editor: Wu Yuezhou
Editorial Director: Zhang Yicong

Senior Consultants: Sun Yong, Wu Ying, Yang Xinci
Managing Director and Publisher: Wang Youbu

ISBN: 978-1-60220-255-9

Address any comments about *The Eaglewood Pavilion* to:

Better Link Press
99 Park Ave
New York, NY 10016
USA

or

Shanghai Press and Publishing Development Company
F 7 Donghu Road, Shanghai, China (200031)
Email: comments_betterlinkpress@hotmail.com

Printed in China by Shenzhen Donnelley Printing Co., Ltd.

1    3    5    7    9    10    8    6    4    2

# THE EAGLEWOOD PAVILION

By Ruan Haibiao
Translated by Wu Xiaozhen

Better Link Press

# Foreword

This collection of books for English readers consists of short stories and novellas published by writers based in Shanghai. Apart from a few who are immigrants to Shanghai, most of them were born in the city, from the latter part of the 1940s to the 1980s. Some of them had their works published in the late 1970s and the early 1980s; some gained recognition only in the 21st century. The older among them were the focus of the "To the Mountains and Villages" campaign in their youth, and as a result, lived and worked in the villages. The difficult paths of their lives had given them unique experiences and perspectives prior to their eventual return to Shanghai. They took up creative writing for different reasons but all share a creative urge and a love for writing. By profession, some of them are college professors, some literary editors, some directors of literary institutions, some freelance writers and some professional writers. From the individual styles of the authors and the art of their writings, readers can easily detect traces of the authors' own experiences in life, their interests, as well as their aesthetic values. Most of the works in this collection are still written in the realistic style that represents, in a painstakingly fashioned fictional world, the changes of the times in urban and rural life. Having grown up in a more open era, the younger writers have been spared the hardships experienced by their predecessors, and therefore seek greater freedom in their writing. Whatever category of writers they belong to, all of them have gained their rightful places in Chinese literary circles over the last forty years. Shanghai writers tend to favor urban narratives more than other genres of writing. Most of the works in this collection can be characterized as urban literature with Shanghai characteristics, but there are also exceptions.

Called the "Paris of the East," Shanghai was already an international metropolis in the 1920s and 30s. Being the center of China's economy, culture and literature at the time, it housed a majority of writers of importance in the history of modern Chinese literature. The list includes Lu Xun, Guo Moruo, Mao Dun and Ba Jin, who had all written and published prolifically in Shanghai. Now, with Shanghai re-emerging as a globalized metropolis, the Shanghai writers who have appeared on the literary scene in the last forty years all face new challenges and literary quests of the times. I am confident that some of the older writers will produce new masterpieces. As for the fledging new generation of writers, we naturally expect them to go far in their long writing careers ahead of them. In due course, we will also introduce those writers who did not make it into this collection.

Wang Jiren
Series Editor

# Contents

# The Eaglewood Pavilion

# I

Why was it called the "Eaglewood Pavilion"? Who was its architect? When was it built? When was it completed? Who used to live here? ... Answers to all these questions are lost forever. The building, like an average senior citizen, has seen nothing memorable despite a long life, yet its age and surroundings are reasons enough for local residents to consider it historical.

There is a peculiar-looking ancient apricot tree about a hundred meters from the Pavilion, which people say General Lu Xun of the Kingdom of Wu planted upon his mother's 80th birthday. Although only part of the tree survives, it thrives, an invariable canopy of luxuriant green with the advent of each spring. Its age stirs up people's fantasies about ancient times, and its figure inspires awe: a stout trunk planted squarely in the earth like the torso of a giant, a huge, unfathomable hole where the giant's bellybutton is supposed to be, two ancient branches poking the sky like an old man who stretched and yawned to relieve the weariness of standing. With a head, the giant's figure would be complete. According to legend, the God of Thunder beheaded the giant for wreaking havoc during a rainstorm. The gap between the two branches was wide enough for a head.

While the peculiar-looking, ancient apricot tree adds mystery to the Eaglewood Pavilion, a more celebrated ancient building three blocks to its west is truly a place of historic interest. That is the memorial to Xu Guangqi, a great scientist and politician in the late Ming Dynasty (1368–1644). Nobody in the neighborhood can tell who built it, and there is no way to find out. During the campaign to do away with the "four olds" (old ideas, old culture, old customs and old habits), intruders spotted the statue of a sparsely-bearded, thin old man wearing a black gauze official's cap, half hidden from view by heavy, apricot-yellow curtains behind a long altar in the main room of the compound's second row of houses. It was believed to be the statue of Xu. Unfortunately, hot-blooded Red Guards smashed it and everything else in the memorial, even though any museum would have welcomed such addition to its collection. The memorial itself was converted into a neighborhood workshop.

During the fervor for folk stories in 1958, Xiao Wei, a young, full-time writer at the District Cultural Center, came to the Eaglewood Pavilion to visit an eighty-year-old lady who was well versed in local anecdotes. She did have plenty of stories worthy of documentation, but she was too old and too hard of hearing to immediately understand what the young man wanted. When she eventually shifted into storytelling mode, Xiao Wei listened attentively, only to recognize some fragments like "long-haired Taiping rebels" (against the Qing Dynasty rulers in the late 1800s, Taiping Heavenly Kingdom soldiers refused to shave their heads) and "Little Mirror." It turned out that the old lady spoke Cantonese, which was Greek to Xiao Wei, a Shandong native. Knowing intuitively that the old lady was a precious walking archive, Xiao Wei decided to bring a recorder the next day and to decipher the stories later. The old lady died unexpectedly that night. Xiao Wei wrung his hands in sorrow. Then he had another idea: Why not chat up the old lady's son? Maybe he had memorized some stories. However, the son was far from obliging. Why? He had been a Taoist priest in the old days. After 1949, his much-heightened political awareness made him determined to make a clean break with his superstitious past. Despite Xiao Wei's appeals, he didn't open up. It was so awkward that others dropped hints at Xiao Wei: In the height of the Small Swords Association Uprising (an armed uprising in Xiamen and Shanghai in 1853), a general nicknamed "Little Mirror" stayed at the Eaglewood Pavilion, and Liu Lichuan, head of the Small Swords Association, visited in the disguise of a medical doctor ... Another former male resident was rumored to run a tofu stall while working undercover for the Communist Party. He didn't leave until after the South Anhui Incident in 1941 and is now holding a key position in the Central Government, but there was no way to ascertain his name ...

The Eaglewood Pavilion fell back into oblivion.

Actually, its exterior is indistinguishable from most other buildings in the Old Town of Shanghai. The age-old tiled rooftop, enlaced with raspberry vines, bears down on a low lintel. A pair of half-broken doors squeak to and fro. Under the eaves hang worn coir brushes, torn baskets held together by cords, half of a pork trotter saved for important occasions, children's red clothes, and girls' multi-colored underwear. However, its interior is a marvel. Anyone who cared to make a model of it could very well enter it into an international competition with the likes of the quadrangle dwellings in Beijing or Master of the Nets Garden in Suzhou, because it fully reflects the extraordinary talent of the Chinese people in maximizing space. For example: Remove a few bricks from the wall, and there is a perfect cupboard; hang several strings of galvanized wire from a beam to suspend a thin plank, and there is a delicate attic.

It's anyone's guess as to whether such the structure should be categorized as masonry-timber, bamboo-timber, or steel-timber. In fact, all building materials, from the primitive ones used by our ancestors to recent inventions, are put to good use here. The structure's existence is justified even if foreigners have no name for it. What is actual is rational. Let foreigners probe it with all their equipment. What they find out about the roof tile, the earth, and the wood grain will only prove what a marvel the Pavilion is. They will be impressed not only by human ingenuity, but also by nature's grand design. Look—rain and snow have washed it over and over, scaffolds prop it up in anticipation of typhoons, termites have left behind latticework, and shrapnel from the Japanese invaders has altered its façade ...

# II

If a composer finds himself inside the Eaglewood Pavilion late at night, he will definitely master the art of orchestration. He will hear heavier snores of men and lighter snores of women, teeth grinding, sleep talking and an occasional sob that escapes the dreamland like a bar from an aria. He will understand perfectly what harmony is. The tone color here rivals that of an Italian-made violin: mild, melodic, enchanting, and lingering, since the wooden partitions have filtered out all the discord. It is said that Niccolo Paganini's violin has perfect intonation because it is made from a century-old Chinese parasol tree. The wooden partitions at the Eaglewood Pavilion are so well aged that they are in no way inferior.

Right now, to the left of a narrow passageway and behind a thin board, someone is snoring as loudly as a steam engine. It must be a man in the prime of life. Indeed, it is Ding Dawei, a thirty-six-year-old man whose snoring is also in its prime. Dawei's snoring jars the symphony at night, and others often complain about it. Dawei is troubled, but he can't find a way to mellow it. Whenever people mention it, he is crestfallen and tongue-tied. However, his wife likes it, especially on winter nights; she claims that it conjures up the image of a blazing furnace and dispels the chill. How come? Dawei brings home the heat of the furnace from the steel mill where he works. Of course this is just a joke. It's common knowledge that the more exhausted one is during the day, the heavier the sleep is at night, and the louder the snoring. Dawei has a tough job, working three shifts as a furnaceman. Tall, big, and fierce, he looks like a model steelworker. His room is hardly big enough to fit him, but somehow he manages to share it with his wife, Tian Xiaoyuan, who is a primary school teacher.

Xiaoyuan has adapted to the environment amazingly well: With the last-quarter moon high above in the sky, she curls up in a faint pool of lamplight in a corner, not the least disturbed by the noises her husband and neighbors make in their sleep, preparing her lessons for tomorrow and grading her students' assignments. People suffering from attention deficit disorder may envy her, but they'd better not, because anyone who lives here for two months will acquire her equanimity.

The fact that Ding Dawei and Tian Xiaoyuan have been married for almost six years without producing any offspring gives rise to speculations. Someone even teased Dawei, "Dawei, they're going to recognize you as a Family Planning Activist!" Dawei knew well enough to play dumb. He scratched his crew cut with his paw and replied cheerfully, "That's flattering! I'm not good enough for such an honor. But if I were married in 1958, I might have become a model parent with at least half a dozen kids. Don't you believe it?" The guy was amused. Ms. Tian, who was quiet and gentle in public, cast her husband a warning glance. She disliked vulgarity. Dawei took the cue. He turned to the guy with a serious look, "Just kidding. To tell you the truth, we don't have any kids because there is just no room!" Ms. Tian cast him a glance of approval. Intellectuals like her know how important it is to bring kids up in the right environment. Mencius' mother moved three times to find the right neighbors. Kids can wait.

While Dawei is the loudest snorer at the Eaglewood Pavilion, the runner-up makes his presence known to the right of the narrow passageway. People can rightly tell it is the noise of someone who indulges in drinking. It is Grandpa Rice Wine, a pensioner. Every evening, he makes a dish to go with his wine—which he sips at leisure—such as spiral shells stir-fried in scallion oil, fried peanuts, or stewed, dried, salted yellow croakers originally from Ningbo. After wining and dining, it's TV time. If a Shaoxing Opera happens to be on air, he sings along, lisping badly. From time to time he inserts some comments in his hometown dialect,

"Crap. What an awful tune!" "The acting sucks!" If he watches a soccer game, he is soon carried away, exclaiming as the ball moves, "Idiot, run for your life!" "Oh my, look out!" If there is neither a Shaoxing Opera nor a soccer game on, he turns off the TV, goes to bed, and snores heartily. If he were younger, his snoring would be as vigorous as Dawei's. But now, considering his snoring has already peaked, people predicted that his daughter-in-law would overtake him soon.

Do women snore, too? Certainly. Snoring is not gender specific. Right now, as Grandpa Rice Wine's loud, tipsy snore falls, his daughter-in-law's softer version rises just a partition away. The father-in-law works out the theme, and the daughter-in-law plays bass. The soothing ensemble puts Baobao, Grandpa Rice Wine's seven-year-old grandson, into such a sweet slumber that he wets his bed. As a result, his mother stops snoring and spanks him out of annoyance. Grandpa Rice Wine cuts short his snoring to scold his daughter-in-law, "Don't. He isn't awake. You will scare the soul out of him."

Everyone else in the house wakes up. Some start to whisper to their bedmate, others take a leak. Alas, can anyone rest well in such an environment? No wonder Caihua—Grandpa Rice Wine's daughter-in-law and Baobao's mother—complains constantly of hypertension, migraine, and shortness of breath. Since summer is the worst, she asks her employer for a long sick leave whenever the weather becomes hot. Her husband—Baobao's father—has gone to work in the hinterlands of China, leaving her and their son to share a room with Grandpa Rice Wine, which is awkward. She has divided the room into two with a partition. While her father-in-law sleeps in the space near the door, she and her son are confined to the inner chamber, where there is only a north-facing window that fails to let in any cool air. Fanning herself throughout the night doesn't help. People have told her she could sleep better on a bamboo couch at the entrance to their lane where there is a draft, but unfortunately, splaying out in public doesn't suit women. "Gosh, this house is like an incinerator," she can't help lamenting. Nevertheless, her mood lifts as soon as summer is over, and she becomes the cheerful person she is predisposed to be once again.

If the snores here give inspiration to musicians, then the sleep talking here is well worthy the study of sociologists. At the Eaglewood Pavilion, Huang Xiaomao, Grandpa Rice Wine's upstairs neighbor, is the champion in that sphere. A deep-lunged, bulky guy in his thirties, Xiaomao sleep-talks throughout the night. Is it a disease? His mother was worried about her only child. According to a veteran doctor of traditional Chinese medicine she consulted, Xiaomao suffers from *yin* deficiency and *yang* excess. While Mrs. Huang leaves no stone unturned in her search for a cure, she finds it quite fascinating to decipher her son's sleep talk in the still of night. As the old saying goes, what you dream about at night reflects what you think about during the day. Xiaomao's sleep talk has evolved with time. A few years ago, when the Red Guards dominated the nation, the young Xiaomao shouted slogans in his dream, "Down with so-and-so! Set so-and-so on fire! Tread enemies underfoot!" Sometimes he stretched out a fist all of a sudden and smashed the porcelain teacup on his nightstand to the floor, which gave neighbors such a start that they thought enemies of the people had invaded the house. More recently, Xiaomao picked up singing in his dreams. Lyrics such as "tasty wine and coffee," "don't pick wild flowers on your path," "oh Mother" put Mrs. Huang's mind at ease: Her son had grown up enough to stay out of trouble. However, nowadays, instead of "oh Mother" she hears grumbles such as, "Will the king date the queen?" or "One can't have a room to marry his woman until his parents die."

Mrs. Huang gets the message at once: Xiaomao wants a wife. In his dream he reveals the innermost thoughts and feelings. Widowed at a young age, she had a hard time raising her son. Of course she'd like to have the family line continued. Young women today are so demanding, whereas the two of them have no other material possession besides this rundown room with creaking floorboards. Mrs. Huang tries to have empathy from time to time: Man struggles upwards, water flows downwards. Hens hatch only after they have built a cozy nest. Girls naturally want a nice home to settle in. Therefore, she often prays for a hurricane, an earthquake, or a lightning strike to destroy the damned house.

Some people disagree: Their room might be shabby, but it has a floor area of more than ten square meters, decent enough to accommodate a newly married couple by prevailing standards. Xiaomao fails to find a wife not because of inadequate housing, but because of his criteria for a future spouse—things like looks, carriage, native place, personality, type of work, and income. Girls, on the other hand, have their eyes on classy men who live in garden houses and have relatives overseas. That's why Xiaomao has never seen eye to eye with any girl, despite his multiple attempts. Mrs. Huang blamed it all on bad luck. She insisted that housing was the key and that she had ample proof.

For example, Aunt Caihua downstairs once tried to set Xiaomao up with a woman in her early thirties who worked at the neighborhood factory that operates from the former Xu Guangqi Memorial. After Mrs. Huang had spied on the woman, she told Caihua, "She is OK, if only her neck could be longer and her face smaller." Caihua was about to retort, but Mrs. Huang added hastily, "It doesn't matter. As long as they are both over thirty, it's time to settle down!" A blind date was arranged. Xiaomao frowned at what he saw. The girl heard about it and sent words over, "Who does he think he is! Just look at his home, freezing in winter, sweltering in summer, and suffocating any other day of the year!" Mrs. Huang drew a long sigh, "Alas, housing, damned housing. When can I have a grandson?" Right away she resumed applying for an audience with higher authorities to appeal for help, an activity she had shelved during the previous summer's heat.

While Mrs. Huang had reason to sigh, another Eaglewood Pavilion resident bore an even greater grievance. Who is that person? Li Guijuan, head of the family next to the Huangs, also known as Mrs. Party Secretary. Why does she go by this name? Her late husband was party secretary of a small restaurant. Mrs. Party Secretary works at a snack bar. She shares a low-ceilinged attic of more than ten square meters with her son and daughter. She sighs heavily whenever the topic of housing comes up. Her husband was said to have met his ill fate because of housing.

At the Eaglewood Pavilion, neighbors are just one thin wall away. And the walls do have ears. There is no privacy at all. Years ago, in the heat of the political movement against reactionary sabotage, graft, theft, speculation, extravagance, and waste, some whistleblower informed the authorities that the newly married Mr. and Mrs. Party Secretary were always counting money up in their attic after work, saying things like "fifty big ones and a hundred small ones."

At that time, class struggle was the big thing. The authorities, suspecting economic crimes, ordered an investigation right away. The head of the investigation team, who was in the good graces of the authorities thanks to his rise against the capitalist and reactionary line, had some old scores to settle with Mr. Party Secretary. Mr. Party Secretary gave confused confessions when threatened. It was only much later into the interrogation that it dawned upon him: The fifties and hundreds the interrogators wanted so much to find out must be from a joke of his wife's, the one about his face pockmarked by smallpox.

The explanation saved his life, but not his health. Repeated public denouncement sessions left him paralyzed. The story may not be entirely true, but Mrs. Party Secretary's sighs are very real. Because she has to rise early for work, she always wants to go to bed right after supper, but with all the TVs, record players, hand clapping, and cheers in the building, she has to resort to sleeping pills. Year in and year out, unlike other women originally from Suzhou, who typically lose their figures after turning forty, she has become a bag of bones. However, her daughter can't get into college on sleeping pills. This high-school girl is gentle, quiet, smart, and motivated. She fights the radio waves and other noises with her strong will. Yet Mrs. Party Secretary fears that her daughter's brain will be jammed by radio waves one of these days … she sighs even more.

Aside from the sighs of Mrs. Party Secretary, there is sometimes wailing at night that sends chills down one's spine. Who wails for his parents in his dream? The former Taoist priest who lives below the Huang family. It is heart wrenching to hear a man in his sixties cry for his parents, isn't it? Don't go soft yet, because he is not tearful at all during the day. His name is Li Rihai. When he was young, he tried many jobs: a rickshaw man, a peddler of salted yellow croaker, a fortuneteller, and a henchman for a police sergeant of the puppet regime, but none agreed with him. As he came down in the world, he was still looking for low-hanging fruit. One day, he squatted in front of his house, doodling in the dirt with a willow branch out of boredom. A passing old Taoist priest from the White Cloud Temple saw what he drew. He approached Mr. Li excitedly, saying, "You have some talent. Come to my temple. Let's have a little talk." Mr. Li accepted the invitation. Shortly afterward, he joined the Taoist priesthood, a profession that required neither physical strength nor intelligence, just the gift of gab. Being no stupid guy, Mr. Li soon excelled in performing Taoist rituals and drawing magic figures to invoke or exorcise spirits. Daily penmanship and arithmetic were a piece of cake for him, too. After the 1949 Liberation, his vocation was abolished. He became head graphic designer at a handkerchief factory, where his talent was so appreciated that he worked well beyond normal retirement age.

One would expect him to laugh in his sleep because the new society made him a respectable citizen, but no, he has his son on his mind, who is retained by the reform-through-labor farm upon completion of a prison sentence. Mr. Li has petitioned for the return of his son. The authorities decided to send an investigator to look into the surroundings where the testy ex-prisoner was to turn a new leaf. A neighbor told the investigator that the young man had gone astray because his home was too small and living conditions too harsh. Mr. Li, the former Taoist priest, knows very well who that ill-wishing neighbor was, but soft as he is, he can't possibly confront the guy during daytime. Instead he mutters curses at night. When he tosses and turns in bed, he thinks aloud angrily, "Bah, what have I done to deserve this?"

Just think what he has done for his neighbors. Like Grandpa Rice Wine's grandson: When he was barely three months old, he was an emaciated weakling who cried throughout the night. Caihua sneaked into his room and begged him to draw some magic figures to exorcise evil spirits. He should have said no, considering the formidable proletariat dictatorship, but he didn't have the heart to. In the end, he risked his life by having Caihua stick a few magic figures to the walls of the men's room. Whether it worked or not, his chivalry should have impressed Caihua and others, right?

And then there is Mrs. Huang upstairs, mother of Huang Xiaomao. Mr. Li even yielded some space on the landing outside his room for her to set up a cooking stove. He is filled with remorse whenever this event comes back to his mind, but soon remorse would be replaced by gratitude. After all, it was Mrs. Huang, a member of the neighborhood proletariat dictatorship taskforce, who turned away the Red Guards who came to fetch him for public denouncement rallies. Before he had recovered from the shock, Mrs. Huang had staked out new territory outside his door. How could he possibly dispute with his benefactor? As a result, Mrs. Huang gained two more square meters' space at his loss … otherwise he could have expanded his room onto the landing and his son could have come home. Mr. Li is constantly tortured by the thought, to the extent that he wails in his sleep.

Inhabitants of the Eaglewood Pavilion certainly find their life inconvenient, but they are still quite contented if there is no extra cause for melancholy. In their minds, the good neighborly spirit makes up for the physical discomfort. Since the walls are thin, a slight moan will put everyone in the house on alert.

Dawei once spoke of it highly, "If there is anything I can tell for sure about this house, that is no one living here will ever die of myocardial infarction, day or night, young or old, out of sorrow or joy." He even quoted a story from the *Reference News* wherein the body of a senior citizen in a foreign country was not discovered until half a year later, contrasting the flimsy human relationship in capitalist society with the harmony among neighbors at the Eaglewood Pavilion. Caihua, who used to play Granny Li in the revolutionary model opera *Red Lantern* for a cultural troupe when she was younger, chimed in with Granny Li's line, "With the wall we're two families; without the wall we're one family!" Everybody exploded with laughter.

Caihua was right. One summer night, Grandpa Rice Wine woke up with a dry throat, thanks to an extra large portion of wine at dinner. As he got up to find his water glass, there was a thud next door. Alerted, he cleared his throat, but not a soul stirred next door. He shook his bedstead violently. Still the squeaking provoked no response at all. He grew concerned: Dawei is on night duty. Has anything gone wrong with Ms. Tian? He almost shouted out but caught himself in time: What if Ms. Tian is all right and gets angry at his shout? At his wit's end, Grandpa Rice Wine bent down, found a crack in the wooden wall, and called in a small voice, "Ms. Tian! Tian Xiaoyuan!" Little did he expect to wake up his daughter-in-law, who crept out of bed to check out on him. What! Has the old man gone crazy? What is he doing in front of that crack deep at night with only a pair of drawers on? Blood rushed into her head. She switched on the fluorescent light and glared.

"What are you doing?" The profoundly wronged father-in-law hurried to explain. Caihua's fury was immediately channeled into action. She rushed out, broke down Dawei's door, and found Ms. Tian unconscious on the floor clutching a student's exercise book! She screamed at the top of her lungs. The entire house was rocked, and Mrs. Huang produced her son's bicycle key. Caihua and Mrs. Party Secretary carried Ms. Tian onto the backseat. Grandpa Rice Wine had the handlebar. Together they hurried towards the hospital. While they were still on their way, the former Taoist priest caught up with them, carrying half a watermelon.

That's why people are reluctant to move away from the Eaglewood Pavilion. Yet most of time, they can't help finding fault with it. Don't get it wrong, though. Criticism drives progress. Good cases in point are the continuous rain in late autumn and thunderstorms in summer. The dripping may sound idyllic when your room is dry, but not when you have to catch leaks with pots and pans. A household of five needs an average of three basins to catch the rain, but at the Eaglewood Pavilion, residents buy as many as their means allow—especially those living upstairs.

Take the Huangs on the second floor, for example. They've got at least a dozen containers of various sizes and materials. Moreover, the former Taoist priest living downstairs contributed a blue-and-white, porcelain, two-eared urn produced in *Guan Kiln* (one of the five famous historical kilns in China) during the reign of Emperor Qianlong of the Qing Dynasty (1644–1911). Why did he contribute it in the first place? Well, Mrs. Huang had a point: People living downstairs are in the same boat as those living upstairs. She laid out her grounds clean and clear— the widely known slogan during the Anti-Japanese War applied in this case, "Let those with money contribute money. Let those with manpower contribute manpower." The former Taoist priest did not argue, but he hated to part with the urn.

It rained incessantly that year. Raindrops wore away the tar felt on the roof. Trickles damaged the interior walls Xiaomao had painstakingly painted. Mrs. Huang mobilized all containers (including the new rage, a pressure cooker), but she was still two vessels short. She moved the camphorwood chest hither and thither, all to no avail. When Xiaomao came home, their new cotton batting was about to be ruined. She told him to hold it while she ran down to borrow some more containers from the former Taoist priest. The latter was a good-natured miser. What?

After occupying the landing outside my door, you want to lay hands on my possessions again? No way! Mrs. Huang swore her way back upstairs.

Xiaomao knit his brows and a stratagem came to mind. Back at primary school, he had read a historical story about how Li Bing and his son built the Dujiang Weir, a hydraulic project in the Warring States Period (475–221 BC). With a kitchen knife, Xiaomao halved a bamboo pole used for hanging wash to dry into a makeshift duct. He held up the duct to catch leakage on one end and poked the other end into a wrist-watch-sized hole in the floorboard.

In the *Legend of the White Snake*, there is a major episode about the flooding of the Jinshan Temple. Madam White Snake fell in love with a mortal named Xu Xian, and they led a happy life together until Monk Fahai saw through Madam White Snake. He hid Xu Xian in Jinshan Temple. The enraged Madam White Snake conjured up water to flood the temple and force Xu Xian out. Now, when Xiaomao directed the water through his floor, the room downstairs was immediately flooded like Jinshan Temple.

Well, the wicked Buddhist monk Fahai inhabited Jinshan Temple, whereas a panicky Taoist priest Rihai took up his quarters downstairs. The latter fled his room, pleaded with the Huangs, and offered up the antique urn—because Mrs. Huang had once commented that the urn preserved pickles even in summer.

Everybody at the Eaglewood Pavilion turned a deaf ear to the incident, except for the hot-blooded steel worker. He waited until an opportunity arose. One day, Bingbing, son of Mrs. Party Secretary, came to seek tutorial from Ms. Tian on how to improve narrative writing. Since Ms. Tian was still at work, Dawei received him. Dawei's compositions had been published in the middle-school newspaper, and he tried his hand at novel writing in his spare time, although nothing had been put to press. Bingbing had always respected Dawei. When Dawei asked him to sit down, he obliged.

"There are three key ingredients to good narrative writing: time, place and character." Dawei narrowed his eyes, thinking. "Take the Eaglewood Pavilion, for example. 'The Spring Festival is around the corner.' That would be the time. Then, 'The Eaglewood Pavilion is immersed in a festive atmosphere. Steam rises from pots and pans, chopsticks click against bowls.' What a lively scene!" Bingbing nodded solemnly. "What about character?" Dawei knitted his brows, "I suggest Grandpa Rice Wine, your downstairs neighbor. Oh, there is a thing between your family and his ... Bingbing, primary school students should learn to think independently. Actually, there are many nice things about Grandpa Rice Wine ... Yes, we'll write about him. Let's start with some description. 'Grandpa Rice Wine is in his sixties. He is stout and bald, with a red, pointy nose like Pinocchio's ...' Oh no, we can't write about his nose. He will think we are making fun of him. Let's find another character. How about Mrs. Huang?" Bingbing nodded agreement. It took Uncle Ding a long time to speak again. When he did, he was clearly worked up.

"Let's write about Li Rihai, the Taoist priest!" Dawei's eyes were lit up. "Bingbing, I want so much to rewrite the *Legend of Madam White Snake*. Monk Fahai was imprisoned under the Leifeng Tower for what he had done. Because he showed clear signs of repentance, the Jade Emperor ordered his early release. Fahai did everything he could to wash away his sin, but Madam White Snake was not appeased. One day, she confronted Fahai again for the return of Xiao Qing, her green snake maid. Fahai told her Xiao Qing had returned to Mount Emei. Madam White Snake pointed at a two-eared urn: This is Xiao Qing! She preserves pickles even in summer!" Bingbing sniggered. Dawei went on with a serious face, "Later, Madam White Snake flooded Fahai again. The poor Fahai had to surrender the two-eared urn. But Madam White Snake didn't turn the urn back into Xiao Qing. She used it to preserve pickles—what logic that is!"

Bingbing stared at Uncle Ding. He'd had meningitis. He

didn't understand why Uncle Ding's face had suddenly reddened all over ...

# III

By nightfall, all residents of the Eaglewood Pavilion have returned home. Food sizzles in pans. Rice boils in cookers.

Despite Mrs. Huang's reputation as a shrewd woman, residents at the Eaglewood Pavilion consider her indispensable, because she always knows what's new. On that day, her trend report started with Xiaomao's jeans, of which she had spoken so often to the largest gatherings in the house that everybody knows the following story by heart: After Xiaomao brought the new pair of jeans home, he soaked it in soap water for three days to give it a used look. Only then did he put it on. He cherished the butter biscuit-sized copper label on the back pocket very much, because it is the very proof of authenticity. The copper label was the highlight of Mrs. Huang's stories. Once, it fell off during washing. She was thankful, because friction damages the fabric. Estimating the weight of the label at about 100 to 150 grams, she made a point to stop in front of Grandpa Rice Wine's door on her way back from the public tap, half talking to herself and half trying to impress the old man, "My! Before Liberation, clerks in foreign banks used to wear a round brass on their breast pocket, the size of a cherry, much smaller than this one. Now people wear it on their behind. I really don't see why." Afterward, she put the label away, together with a scrapped Bullhead Brand spring lock, planning to sell both to the rags-and-bone man someday. Hardly did she expect the hell her son was going to raise the same night when he pulled on the jeans for a blind date only to find the copper label missing. Without it, others would think the jeans were fake! Xiaomao was furious: He had paid more than 30 yuan (approximately 6 US dollars) not for the jeans, but for the label! By the time Mrs. Huang fumbled out the label, Xiaomao was due to leave. There was no time to sew it back on. He refused to go on the date. Mrs. Huang pleaded and pleaded, her eyes red-rimmed. Finally, Xiaomao relented. He didn't tuck his shirt into the jeans like he usually did, to draw attention to the bulging pants seat and the brass plate. Instead, he let it drape over the jeans.

"We are too old to understand foreigners or foreign stuff . . ." This is her lead-in to the story of the day. On that afternoon, her nap was interrupted by light footsteps downstairs. They were not any neighbor's. Who could it be? She pricked up her ears. Then she heard faint voices. Were enemies of the people in the house? She got up, found her shoes, dashed downstairs. How weird! Two blond foreigners, an old man and an old woman, were directing a dark, ominous object at the Eaglewood Pavilion. There was a click followed by a flash, then another click, and another flash . . . what was going on?! Were they trying to set the house on fire? Mrs. Huang shouted, "Hey you, what are you doing?" The foreigners were not scared at all. On the contrary, they advanced into the Eaglewood Pavilion pointing the long object at her. Click click, flash flash. Mrs. Huang felt dizzy and something tingled in her chest. No, it was not very painful, but the tension made her fall to the floor. Recalling shootouts in movies, she did a quick self-check. Eh, why wasn't there blood? Then she realized she was not dead at all!

. . .

It's hard to say how much of Mrs. Huang's story was true, but it's enough to start a debate among inhabitants of the Eaglewood Pavilion.

"It must be a rocket launcher! She said it was long and round. What else can it be?!" Grandpa Rice Wine, who was at a teahouse when the two foreigners invaded the Eaglewood Pavilion, fires away immediately because otherwise neighbors may shush him by quoting the famous dictum, "He who makes no investigation and study has no right to speak." Mrs. Huang's expression is inscrutable. Her usual response to Grandpa Rice Wine's comments was, "Old tippler, stop babbling!" This time she doesn't retort. How she wishes it were a rocket launcher—even if she has no idea what a rocket launcher is. Why? Don't you need fire to launch a rocket? If the "rocket launcher" spits fire, she and Xiaomao would be lifted out of misery!

"Are you sure? Why didn't the long object spit fire after the flash?" It took her a long time to come up with a challenge to Grandpa Rice Wine, and she did so only because she wanted to be convinced. Then her wish could come true …

Caihua is amused by the argument back and forth between the two elders. To hell with the rocket launcher. You might as well call it a long-range missile! But she catches herself before speaking out. Xiaomao's mother has hypertension. What if she gets all worked up and suffers a stroke? However, the two old sillies simply can't stop the gibble-gabble. She puts down the slice.

"Hear, hear, a rocket launcher! I wish it exploded, burned down the Eaglewood Pavilion, and killed a lot of us … what's wrong with you guys? Let me tell you. It was a camera, not a rocket launcher. The flashes came from the flashlight!"

Mrs. Huang is taken aback. How dare Caihua to reduce the ominous object to a commonplace camera!

"Humph, a camera!" She is not humored, "Caihua, do you think I'm a hick and have never seen a camera? Let me tell you this. Xiaomao has many hobbies. He takes pictures and develops photos for many girls … I've seen his cameras. None of them gives off white light."

Hardly has her voice faded away before Grandpa Rice Wine cackles. To be fair, he doesn't do so to ridicule Mrs. Huang. He is happy for himself. His daughter-in-law is stir-frying some spiral shells in scallion oil, which goes very well with rice wine. Since Caihua fusses over the amount of wine he drinks for health reasons, he has been on the lookout for ways to please her. Here comes an opportunity! He speaks to Mrs. Huang in a disdainful tone.

"Xiaomao's camera is a far cry from what the foreigners had!" At a side-glance he catches a faint smile on Caihua's face.

Emboldened, he declares that Xiaomao has only one camera, not many, as claimed by Mrs. Huang, and the one camera was bought from a second-hand shop! Grandpa Rice Wine sounds like he's passing judgment. Mrs. Huang bristles with indignity. She was not affronted when the foreigners clicked and flashed at her, but now she is really pissed off. She hurtles one sarcastic comment after another at the old man: Oh yes, Xiaomao was born under an unlucky star and grew up poor. She herself has fared no better, widowed since a young age and living on the thirty-odd bucks paid by the neighborhood factory. Xiaomao has never seen a Model 246 camera, let along bought one.

Grandpa Rice Wine should know better than to correct Mrs. Huang, but he can't help himself, "Mrs. Huang, you must be mistaken. There is no Model 246 camera in the world, only Model 135."

He is right. Mrs. Huang did mistake her son's Model 135 camera for Model 246. But who can blame her? She is just a housewife. Now she is even angrier.

"Oh yeah, 135, 246, aren't you becoming 768594, you tippler?" This is no raving. This is an encoded curse. What is the sum of seven and six, eight and five, nine and four? Thirteen, right? In the Shanghai slang, the number thirteen stands for the greatest insult. Caught between an angry Mrs. Huang and a sullen Caihua, Grandpa Rice Wine almost bites his tongue off. How simple-minded he was to try to shut up the garrulous Mrs. Huang in order to get a more generous pouring of wine from his daughter-in-law. Caihua drops the slice into the pan with a bang.

"Already tipsy? Time for supper." She picked up the bowl of well stir-fried spiral shells and marched towards home, cursing, "This hypertension is killing me! He just can't stop playing nuts!"

The empty pan shrieks on the stove. Caihua won't allow him more wine tonight. Grandpa Rice Wine is regretful. He should have stopped after the comment on the second-hand shop. That way there wouldn't be any debate over "135" or "246," and Caihua's smile could have lasted until supper. He removes the pan sullenly. It feels even worse when he catches sight of the small, marinated fish on the chopping board. Caihua was too angry to finish cooking.

Dawei comes to his rescue. The bang of the slice against the pan got him out of bed. In fact, he had been lying awake—the bed felt cozy after the night shift. The debate between Grandpa Rice Wine and Mrs. Huang amused him at first, but then he felt sad. The Chinese have enough trouble of their own. Why bother with foreign cameras? Is it in their place to discuss missiles or rockets? They can hardly breathe in this house. Why add more burden to their backs? Seriously, he felt sorry for them, especially Mrs. Huang. She may not have manners, she may be a shrewd woman, but she spoke out the truth. Who would wish to burn down the Eaglewood Pavilion if there is any other alternative? Well, he'd better give these old people something to look forward to!

Since Dawei subscribes to six or seven newspapers, he is very knowledgeable: From UFOs to test-tube babies, from the weight issue of Tonga's prime minister to rectal cancer afflicting a foreign president, from international relations to economic updates and the latest disarmament talks, you just name it. On this occasion he gives those in the shared kitchen a bi-annual review of the construction trends in and out of China reported by the *Municipal Construction*, which he perused issue by issue.

"Actually, once the redevelopment project starts, it takes very little time to build new houses. Nowadays they can build a story a day, and a twenty-four-story Park Hotel in thirty days." Seeing the disbelief in Grandpa Rice Wine's eyes, he adds hastily, "Of course, thirty work days. Construction workers take Sundays off! Building technologies are very advanced now. In the past, houses were built brick by brick. Now, with frame structures, modular structures, sliding formwork, prefab factories, and all that other stuff, everything can be prefabricated. You just haul the ready-made beams, doors, windows, bathtubs, and toilets to the construction site. Then, at the cue of a whistle, you just assemble them. It's a piece of cake to build a story a day, or a house a day. A street a day, that's something!" He babbles as he brushes his teeth, froth all over his mouth.

A moment ago, Grandpa Rice Wine was upset because there was not going to be any fish at supper. Now Dawei cheers him up. As Dawei talks about how two oriental travellers got lost somewhere in Yugoslavia because a new city had sprung up overnight, he slaps himself on the head. Hey, what a dotard I've become! How can I forget such important news?! Yes, I'll tell them now and everyone will be happy.

"Dawei!" His booming voice chops Dawei's verbal torrent off. Dawei stops mid-sentence to regard him doubtfully. Grandpa Rice Wine stares him without uttering another word. Finally, satisfied with the effect of suspense, he lowers his voice.

"Dawei, have you heard of it?"

"What?"

"It's about our house. Redevelopment ..." He coughed convulsively. This is an old trick of his. People's interest in him will only grow stronger if he intersperses an important message with coughs. It's tantalizing. Knowing him well, Dawei makes to return home. Then and only then does Grandpa Rice Wine let the bomb drop. "Our house is earmarked for redevelopment!"

"What!" Dawei stops dead.

"It's real. The entire neighborhood, between this road and that, will be demolished ..." There is not a trace of uncertainty in his tone, as if the Director of the Urban Construction Bureau had submitted a report to him.

People are immediately drawn to such well-founded news. Mrs. Huang, who was on her way to take out garbage, bounds down the stairs. Caihua comes back to the kitchen after listening for a while from her room. Grandpa Rice Wine is delighted to see his mollified daughter-in-law. He recounts what he heard at the teahouse with greater gusto: How the Japanese are to help the Chinese build new houses, how big the new houses will be, and how bulldozers will knock down old buildings. "By that time, everything will be razed to the ground … the world knows how smart and capable the Japanese are. The houses they build will certainly be first-rate. Wait and see. All apartments will be equipped with flush toilets, gas pipelines, and bathtubs. Maybe there will be elevators, too …" Grandpa Rice Wine narrows his eyes in pleasure. His body sways slightly as if he were taking an elevator.

"Elevators make you dizzy. People with high blood pressure will die!" Mrs. Huang chipped in anxiously. Grandpa Rice Wine's vision is so enticing that she hugs the garbage like treasure.

"Die!" Caihua darts a contemptuous look at Mrs. Huang, "Are you too dead to think? Can't you just live on the second or third floor?" She is having high blood pressure. Maybe Mrs. Huang said so to curse her after the camera controversy.

"Right so." Mrs. Huang is eager to please, "People can't live in midair. If our feet don't touch the ground, we die! Mr. Xu in Lane 96 across the street was always in ruddy health. But only a week after moving to a sixth-floor apartment in Pudong, he died!" It doesn't matter that nobody there knows Mr. Xu. She doesn't plan to discuss him anyway. What really concerns her is the Japanese practice of demolition. "Do we remove furniture before bulldozers come?"

"Why bother with the trash! There will be air-conditioning in our new apartments. The government will issue us furniture. Robots will take care of housework. All that is left for us to do is to eat well, sleep well, take a walk in the garden, do some exercise—there will be gardens on the rooftop as well as on the ground," Dawei remarks smilingly before heading home.

Mrs. Huang purses her lips in displeasure. Did Dawei just ridicule her? It was so unmanly. She dismisses him with a grunt. "Take your time and enjoy!" It's time to go, but Caihua speaks again.

"That's nothing. The Japanese have all kinds of household appliances …" Humph, the Japanese again! Mrs. Huang thinks angrily: Why can't you talk about us Chinese? Caihua sounds like a Japanese! If the Japanese didn't help with redevelopment, she would really like to confront Caihua.

"If you admire the Japanese so much, why not marry a Japanese man and move to Japan?"

In the end, Mrs. Huang loses her temper. She even hits another person.

Bingbing, the son of Mrs. Party Secretary, got to know the Japanese from such anti-Japanese-War-themed movies as *Tunnel Warfare* and *Landmine Warfare*. When he comes home after school, the adults are talking about the Japanese. The Japanese, he thinks to himself—the warriors who charge unhesitatingly with swords slung over their shoulders, wearing caps with a sun-shaped insignia! In his childish mind, he admires all military men—even military villains.

When Grandpa Rice Wine mentions how the Japanese are going to help the Chinese build houses, he is filled with deeper esteem for them. Auntie Caihua's remarks shape their images into perfection. He claps his hands and whoops, "The Japanese are great. The Japanese are mighty, mightier than the Americans!" Then he gets two knuckles on the head. Slightly dizzy, he turns around to see who the culprit is. It is a disgusted Mrs. Huang.

"Humph, you little rogue. Don't you know manners? If the Japs come, we'll see how they beat the crap out of you!" Bingbing is baffled, but he dare not challenge the ferocious-looking old lady. He climbs the stairs, muttering to himself.

Caihua feels sorry for the frail, fatherless boy. She wants to reprove Mrs. Huang, but on second thought, Mrs. Huang's anger was justified. Back then, she suffered at the hands of Japanese invaders. According to her recounting at a neighborhood rally, Japanese soldiers frisked both her and Xiaomao's father when they came to Shanghai for the first time as travelling traders. Xiaomao's father was a bit slower than ordered, and they beat him up. She tried to protect him, and the Japs humiliated her. If you were in her shoes, what would you think? No wonder she is disappointed with her fellow Chinese for seeking help from the former aggressors. The Japanese are mighty. Why can't we Chinese be mighty? For the first time, Caihua understands the power of empathy ...

# IV

The bomb dropped by Grandpa Rice Wine created quite a sensation, but life goes back to the usual track after the smoke clears. The intelligence he gathered at the teahouse caused a spat—Mrs. Party Secretary had a word with Mrs. Huang over the bruise on Bingbing's head. His minute of glory as press officer is over. Nobody pays him further attention, although he was very faithful in the news briefing. The loneliness seems to grow on him whenever he is out of the teahouse. Luckily, he has rice wine.

One day, he sets up a small, square table in the passageway and starts to drink by himself. After just one gulp of rice wine, warmth starts to radiate from his navel, like a telegraph-emitting light wave in a postal service poster; after two gulps, the tendon underneath the root of his tongue comes to life like a piston, ready to drive a machine named talking. However, there is no one around to talk to. How lonely he is! It's such a relief to see Mrs. Huang back from another petition trip to the authorities.

He calls out, "Did you go to the Housing Management again? Xiaomao is thirty-four, isn't he? Yes, he was born in the Year of the Dragon. Gosh, he isn't young anymore." Mrs. Huang usually ignores such remarks, but this time her leaden legs seem unable to carry her tired soul any farther. At least Grandpa Rice Wine cares. She sits down on a stool indicated by Grandpa Rice Wine.

"Is Xiaomao seeing anyone?" He takes a contented sip at his wine, "Is it the girl in a dancing gown last night? I knew at once. Otherwise, Xiaomao wouldn't show her the stairs with a flashlight and talk to her for another hour at the entrance.

Young people nowadays seem to have a lot to talk about. In soap operas, they are either chasing one another or talking nonstop. We were not like that in the past. We had other things on our minds! A year after the wedding, we didn't speak more than three sentences to each other any one time … but children arrived quickly! What matters in love are not words, but action. By the way, Mrs. Huang, you should know better than to stick around. Next time when Dancing Gown comes, you just take a walk outside. In this way they'll become closer, and next spring you'll hand out red-dyed boiled eggs …"

Grandpa Rice Wine enjoys himself too much to sense Mrs. Huang's embarrassment. Gosh. He wishes for a new baby next spring! It's hard to catch a hen, let alone a wife! Do you know who the woman last night is? She is Xiaomao's boss, the workshop manager! She graced their messy attic with her presence because Xiaomao had failed to focus on work and produced scraps. They stood talking because Xiaomao must give a decent version of self-criticism … what a wiseass the old man is! Despite these thoughts crossing her mind, Mrs. Huang doesn't have the nerve to tell the truth.

"It's not what you think. She is a princess and Xiaomao is a toad. She lives in a twenty-story mansion near the Shanghai Stadium, but we live in an attic where you can hardly stand up straight. You're daydreaming!" she sighs heavily.

Grandpa Rice Wine nods in apparent sympathy as he relishes the wine, but to make merry he must speak more. He cuts in as Mrs. Huang sighs, "Oh yes, an apartment is key to carrying on the family line. But you don't always need an apartment to make babies. Let them take a steamer to Ningbo. Not berths in the third-class cabin, just a shared bed in the fifth-class cabin. Tell them to get under the blanket when the steamer leaves Wu Song Kou. The waves out on the sea will cover for them! Oh, send them to a park. Oh, oh, after 10 p.m. the day before yesterday, the guard dog at a park barked in front of a grotto entrance. The patrol party turned on their flashlights. What did they see? A naked couple! Do you know what were they doing? They were having sex! The patrol party demanded their ID—it is a crime to have sex in the park! The couple showed them their marriage license! ... Mrs. Huang, that's what young people do nowadays."

"Ugh!" Mrs. Huang frowns as if she had eaten an odd-tasting bean. She feels for the couple, but she would never allow her son to disgrace the family in such a way. She doesn't know what to think or say, as if the couple caught in the torchlight were Xiaomao and his elusive girlfriend.

Among bosom friends, a thousand cups of wine are too few. Before he knows it, Grandpa Rice Wine has drunk more than his daughter-in-law allows. The transparent liquid is now flowing in his body. The tip of his nose, his face, and the whites of his eyes have turned red. He is a boatman drifting in the river of intoxication. How often can a person drink to his heart's content while having someone to talk to? He narrows his eyes in contentment and eyes up the ill-at-ease Mrs. Huang. The shrewd woman seems to stand in awe of him. Exhilarated, he tells Mrs. Huang more stories he heard at the teahouse: Two brothers in their thirties fought over a small room because both wanted to get married in it. In the end, the younger brother killed the older brother. How tragic! A man in his twenties wanted the family anteroom to get married in. His parents hesitated. He put rat poison in their food. Another man who failed to find a girlfriend for lack of a room to get married in went out to stalk women every night. He ended up in prison ...

Grandpa Rice Wine's stories hurt Mrs. Huang like stings. It takes her a long while to realize that the old man is gloating! She explodes, "All those tall tales! You've drunk too much for your own good!"

Grandpa Rice Wine is offended, naturally. "For my own good? No! These stories are for your own good!"

"To hell with you!" Mrs. Huang jumps to her feet and lets loose a stream of abuse at Grandpa Rice Wine, pointing a finger at the latter's liver-colored nose. She is mad at him, and her language is indeed harsh on the ear. Grandpa Rice Wine literally wilts in front of her—his tongue has grown thick and his head swims—Mrs. Huang finds a vent for her pent-up anger at the authorities, the Housing Management, Xiaomao, and herself. When she is done, she shrugs and goes upstairs with much lighter steps.

All the while, Caihua was doing some needlework in her room. Mrs. Huang's remarks pierced her eardrum like needles in her hand. Several times she was on the verge of retorting and then held herself back. That old drunkard needed to be taught a lesson. When she finally can't bear it any longer and storms out, she immediately sees why the old man has been shooting off his mouth. The wine bottle is almost empty! It should have lasted until the fifth of next month. She flares up and grabs the bottle.

Mrs. Huang's verbal abuse has sobered Grandpa Rice Wine up. Remorse has crept into his mind. However, when Caihua grabs the wine bottle, he is so offended that he tries to take it back. Caught by surprise, Caihua lets the bottle slip from her hand. Seeing the puddle of wine scattered with chips of glass, Grandpa Rice Wine flames up. The entire Eaglewood Pavilion may catch fire. Caihua has seldom seen him so angry since she became head of the household. However, since she believes in tit for tat, by no means will she back off.

Ms. Tian, who spent the whole day instilling reason into pupils, has to appeal to the two adults' sense of reason as soon as she comes home. Still angry, Caihua went back to her mother's, taking Baobao with her. Grandpa Rice Wine knows he was in the wrong, yet instead of showing remorse, he finds an empty soy sauce bottle, goes to the grocery store, and has it filled with hard liquor. Back at home, he takes one gulp after another. By and by his tongue stiffens ...

This has been a wet fall. After supper, Dawei leans against the gate watching the rain. A walk outside is impossible. How can he kill time? The aroma of liquor wafts into his nose.

Remembering his wife's report of how Grandpa Rice Wine fell out with his daughter-in-law, he takes a deep breath and strolls to Grandpa Rice Wine's room. The old man is drinking by himself. Even Lu Zhishen in *All Men Are Brothers* would get drunk if he downed the liquor as quickly as Grandpa Rice Wine, Dawei says to himself. At the sight of a friendly face, Grandpa Rice Wine starts to sing a tuneless excerpt from a Ningbo opera while boxing his own ears with both hands. Dawei hurries to remove the wine cup. Grandpa Rice Wine wails and stamps his feet. Suddenly he crashes to the floor, his face all bloated up. The term "alcohol poisoning" crosses Dawei's mind! He shouts out for his wife. The two of them rush the old man to the hospital. Doctors give him an enema. He is fine.

Dawei's mind is in turmoil as he sits by the bed of the soundly sleeping Grandpa Rice Wine while the cold rain pelts the window. Can you blame old people like him? They may have failings, a short temper, and sometimes a foul mouth or bad manners, but what they have experienced is lamentable. High hopes keep them awake at night. Then comes the crush. Once, twice, thrice … their nerves have been worn thin, and so has their patience.

Take this old man in the hospital bed as an example. He used to sleep in a niche for a statue at the City God's Temple. In 1956, with the Chinese economy improving, the government launched a great number of infrastructure projects. Gravel roads were paved with tar. Multi-storied residential buildings sprang up in shantytowns. Even public toilets were rebuilt with reinforced concrete. He longed day and night for reconstruction to start at the Eaglewood Pavilion. However, since the house was located right at the heart of the city, the authorities hesitated over an open-heart surgery. Later, the entire nation got carried away in setting up backyard furnaces for smelting steel. The redevelopment project was shelved. When the Three Years of Natural Disasters were finally over, hope stirred in his heart again, but the Cultural Revolution kicked off all of a sudden. He prayed for a gale to tear the Eaglewood Pavilion off the ground, and a lucky break finally materialized.

Back then, Grandpa Rice Wine, whose ancestors were either farmhands or factory workers, was a hauler at a cement plant. The local rebel faction singled him out because, with a stout figure and a ruddy face, he was the perfect image of a working-class man. They asked him to take over the "realm of the superstructure." He refused. They thought he didn't want to go for fear that he couldn't drink afterward, so they gave him special permission to carry a flask in his red book bag. He again turned them down. The rebel faction leaders were confused. They stressed to him that this was about loyalty to the revolution. He blurted out his grievance: Why should he build a "superstructure" for others when he lives in miserable conditions? "If you really want me to build one, build it to replace the Eaglewood Pavilion!" Of course, Grandpa Rice Wine was mistaken. The so-called "superstructure" was ideological, not physical. Luckily, this was not a matter of principle.

The same night, he gave his neighbors an exaggerated version of what had happened to him over a cup of wine. To his surprise, others put on a serious face instead of looking amused. Caihua, just married at that time, broke the awkward silence.

"Dad, you should bargain with them. Either give us a new apartment or forget about it!" A new apartment? You're demanding a sky-high price indeed. Two rooms in a *shikumen* house will be good enough. Grandpa Rice Wine raised his chopsticks to dismiss his daughter-in-law. At that time, he was still respected by his family.

Mrs. Huang spoke up. As a member of the neighborhood proletariat dictatorship taskforce, she felt obliged to enlighten Grandpa Rice Wine. She advised the latter to look beyond the Eaglewood Pavilion and have the entire world in view. Three-quarters of the world's population were still suffering, including his neighbors at the Eaglewood Pavilion. She made herself very clear: If you want to move out, make sure we move out too.

Otherwise, don't even think about it. This was a sermon on "the emancipation of the entire mankind," so how could Grandpa Rice Wine say no?

Consequently, he repeated her sermon to the rebel faction leaders at his factory the next morning, demanding the reconstruction of the Eaglewood Pavilion. This made things difficult for the leaders. There was plenty of cement at the factory, but many other materials were needed for the reconstruction. Was he trying to hijack the revolution? After some deliberation, they decided not to send Grandpa Rice Wine to take over the superstructure. From then on, the revolutionary forces excluded Grandpa Rice Wine, and he had a good time convening a one-man Revolutionary Committee on Wine Drinking. This exclusion turned out to have a silver lining, because years later he was not implicated in the dissolution of those rebel factions.

The lucky break came and went. Residents at the Eaglewood Pavilion waited patiently for another favorable turn. The Ninth Party Congress, the Tenth Party Congress, the crackdown on the Gang of Four. Any tiny move at the top of the country was received with anticipation, followed by disheartenment and finger pointing. Here is another example—after decades, it is still on some residents' minds, and Li Rihai, the former Taoist priest, is still blamed.

On the day when the Ninth Party Congress concluded, there was a deafening sound of gongs, drums and firecrackers. Before the Ninth Party Congress, people had looked forward to it. While the Ninth Party Congress was convening, people looked forward to its closing, as if upon closing national affairs and domestic affairs alike would turn for the better. Otherwise, why did they do the Yangko dance so merrily? On that day, all the residents of the Eaglewood Pavilion—except Dawei, who was beating a huge drum with nine other guys on Nanjing Road—gathered in the passageway after joining the parade in the streets. Maybe it was the Chinese custom to have an ideological discussion over a major historical event, or maybe they all needed to prepare supper. As usual, they all had opinions to air, and their discussion soon got heated. Grandpa Rice Wine joined the discussion under the influence of the 150 milliliters of Qibao Liquor he had already drunk in honor of the joyous occasion. Caihua fell into a reverie and painted for everyone who cared to listen a rosy picture of the future Eaglewood Pavilion: balconies, curtains with floral patterns, red carpets, flowers in vases ... However, Mrs. Huang thought her "vision" pertained to spawn of feudalism, capitalism, and revisionism. Since it was camaraderie to point out others' mistakes, she immediately offered Caihua some well-intended "criticism." Caihua was defiant, because she had joined her factory's propaganda team and considered herself politically correct. They started to quote Marxist classics to prove their respective points. Before enemies of the people made inroads into the Eaglewood Pavilion, infighting broke out.

Something burned and flames raged over a stove. Damn! Caihua was so into the debate that she had forgotten the frying pan. The draught had sent the fire roaring and the oil in the pan had caught fire! Grandpa Rice Wine scrambled to put out the fire, but either intoxication or confusion made him pour a kettle of water over the pan. With a loud hiss, the fire leapt into the air. Caihua froze, and Mrs. Huang yelled, "Help!"

In the blink of an eye, a door whose paint had peeled off was pushed open. A man in black rushed in. With a lowered head and without uttering a sound, he nimbly picked up a lid and put it over the pan. There was a slight puff, and then thick fumes. The fire was put out. What a narrow escape! A chorus of voices thanked the intrepid hero in black. Even Mrs. Huang, member of the neighborhood proletariat dictatorship taskforce, forgot that this man was an object of dictatorship and shook his hand.

Afterward, Li Rihai, the former Taoist priest, held his lowly head higher, thinking he had earned respect for his bravery. To his shock, some neighbors didn't appreciate his heroic act at all. Instead, one of them said he had put his finger in another's pie. Bloody hell!

"I'd rather let the fire burn. Burn down the house and we can all benefit ..."

What's wrong with you people! If you had burned down the house upon the conclusion of the Ninth Party Congress, you'd be in prison now! The former Taoist priest ground his teeth in anger, but he knew better than to show it in public. In fact, Caihua had made the comment in a fit of pique. She didn't really mean it. Yet the former Taoist priest had lost his sense of humor after all the hardship he had gone through.

# V

Whenever he feels like it, Grandpa Rice Wine gets drunk. Whenever he gets drunk, he makes a scene. Whenever he makes a scene, he is rushed to the hospital. Whenever he is discharged from the hospital, he picks up the wine bottle again. He has named his rice wine the "Revival Wine," as if without it, his soul would not be lured back into his body. After many trips to the hospital, Caihua has come to terms with her father-in-law's ritual of "revival."

Dawei disapproves of Caihua's passivity. In his mind, wine and liquor deprive people of reason. They bring turmoil to the world. All disputes at the Eaglewood Pavilion that involved Grandpa Rice Wine also involved wine. He always peddled leftover tea leaves from the teahouse to neighbors when he was drunk. This time is no different.

However, Dawei is wrong this time. Grandpa Rice Wine told the truth: The neighborhood factory operating from the former Xu Guangqi Memorial is relocating, and the peculiar-looking ancient apricot tree has been identified as a municipal-level cultural relic.

Mrs. Huang sets about investigating immediately—the young woman who almost became her daughter-in-law works at the neighborhood factory, anyway. Soon afterward, she runs into her in the wet market. The young woman recognizes Mrs. Huang, although she seems to have no recollection of Xiaomao. She confirms that her factory is relocating to Pudong. She also mentions that the opinions of her colleagues, who live near the current location, vary. She sounds sad, because it might further hinder her endeavor to find a husband. In contrast, Mrs. Huang is in high spirits. Thank God this girl has not become her daughter-in-law, otherwise it would kill her to cross the Huangpu River every day to babysit her grandson. What's more, if the former Xu Guangqi Memorial is to be restored, how long will it take for redevelopment to happen to the Eaglewood Pavilion three blocks away? ...

Inhabitants of the Eaglewood Pavilion are agitated once more.

It has grown dark. Supper is ready, but they seem to have lost their appetites. Are they ill? No, they are in sound health. Caihua speaks for all of them: You have three meals a day all your life, but news like this breaks only once in a blue moon!

Grandpa Rice Wine again triggers their discussion that day. Although he has not had a drink that day, he sounds tipsy, "... When I was little, just a few years older than Bingbing is right now, there was this boxwood door leaf engraved with deities. Yes, deities from *The Legend of Deification*. The Taoist Deity Li with a miniature pagoda on his palm, and his son Nezha on Wind Fire Wheels with a white lotus flower growing out of his navel ... the all-black, majestic-looking Zhang Yide grabbing a lance ..."

Anyone who has a rudimentary knowledge of history can tell he is talking nonsense. Zhang Yide, also known as Zhang Fei, is a character in the *Romance of the Three Kingdoms*, not a deity in *The Legend of Deification*. However, they are too hungry for new information to care. Moreover, they know Grandpa Rice Wine well enough to wait patiently for the prelude to be over. Sure enough, Grandpa Rice Wine switches to the subject of the day. "By the way, Mrs. Huang, did you see a wooden board when you were married into this house? It's no ordinary board, but a horizontal inscribed board. Do you see what I mean?! ..."

Mrs. Huang is offended. She knows the board very well. It is serving as a floor joist in her attic. There is nothing unusual about it. However, for caution's sake, she is not going to acknowledge its existence today. She doesn't like the way the old man talked about her "marrying into this house." Hum! Flaunting your seniority in front of me? When you fled famine in Ningbo and arrived in Shanghai, I had already been taken into this house by the Huang family as a child bride. "Never heard of it." She puckers her mouth peremptorily, "I do remember an iron furnace. Long-haired Taiping rebels used it to forge swords and spears. After their defeat, our ancestors turned it into a cooking stove ... " She sounds much glibber than Grandpa Rice Wine.

"An iron furnace? Oh yes, I remember it. Mrs. Huang, what happened to it?" Grandpa Rice Wine brightens up. The furnace may be an asset in the current circumstances!

"Ask yourself!" Mrs. Huang's face has gone a bit rigid. Grandpa Rice Wine blinks in confusion. "Who carted it off in 1958?" Mrs. Huang is indignant. Stop pretending! Had it not been for the furnace, you would never have been recognized as activist in the Great Leap Forward Movement, or become a full-time employee at the cement plant!

Thus daunted by Mrs. Huang, Grandpa Rice Wine recalls vaguely how he broke a sweat moving the furnace. What a pity! If it were still here, the Eaglewood Pavilion's historical status might be elevated to something comparable to the Tianyi Pavilion, which was built in the Ming Dynasty (1561) in Ningbo City, Zhejiang Province—the oldest private library in China with a collection of 300,000 volumes, 80,000 of which are rare books.

Caihua is younger and thinks deeper. She sees no point arguing over trifling things. In order to ease the tension, she suggests that they contact the competent authorities. To her surprise, others enthuse. Soon, a plan to turn around the Eaglewood Pavilion is developed. No stone is to be left unturned in its implementation. They must do research to illustrate the

Eaglewood Pavilion's cultural and historical significance.

It is an arduous task, but inhabitants of the Eaglewood Pavilion are tenacious. They make a discovery the same day:

"Hello, Uncle Li!" a sweet charming voice calls out. "You're home!"

The former Taoist priest is so surprised by Caihua's greeting that he stands motionless. It has been a long time since people addressed him in such a manner.

"Yes, yes." He looks blankly at the Caihua's radiant face, not knowing what to expect.

"Hey you, come over!" Mrs. Huang raises her voice. His lukewarm response may have kicked in Mrs. Huang's combative mood. Although the neighborhood proletariat dictatorship taskforce was dissolved long ago, her peculiar tone still causes conditioned reflex in him.

"What, what's up?" There is a buzz in his head and a cramp in his calves. He stares at her like a trapped beast, blinking rapidly. Surprise! What comes into sight is not the usual scornful, thin, flat face, but an obsequious, smiling one.

"Did your mother die in 1958?"

"Hum," his voice sounds as if muffled by polyform.

"Before her death, the government sent a young man to visit her, right?!"

"A young man? I have forgotten. No. Sorry." He has picked up a mantra in the succession of political movements, which is "I have forgotten." He uses it to ward off any question the answer to which he is unsure of or might offend people. It has been very effective in keeping him out of trouble. "Nineteen fifty-eight. It was so long ago. Who has such a long memory?"

"I do!" Mrs. Huang sounds resolute and decisive. The former Taoist priest used to be an object of the proletariat dictatorship. She knows his tactics like the back of her hand. She says to herself, "How dare you to dodge my question with 'I have forgotten'! I'll make you recall every detail!" Thus determined, she fires off, "It was a short young man wearing a pair of glasses over his dark, square face. He carried a handbag. From it he took a leather case. He zipped open the case to take out a box. He unclasped the box to take out a letter of introduction ..." She picks up speed and her voice rises as she continues as if reciting a tongue twister. The expression on her face seems to say, "Ha, you slippery fellow, I've got you!"

Li Rihai, the former Taoist priest, is taken aback. Is it another unlucky day? He ponders. Then his heart plummets and his limbs grow cold.

"Right," he chatters. "What did he say? My mother didn't talk much. Soon after he left, she couldn't breathe because of phlegm, and then she ... passed away ..."

"Did she really not talk much?"

"Did she mention long-haired Taiping rebels?"

"And swords, small swords ..."

His neighbors all talk at once. What swords?! His handbag drops to the floor. What is going on? What does everybody interrogate him? Is another political movement coming? He shivers. Caihua gives a timely explanation. Without it, the jittery Taoist priest might very well have a fit of epilepsy. "Oh ..." he sighs a long sigh of relief and pulls up his trousers. His armpits are wet.

Caihua's friendliness seems genuine. Neighbors look at him expectantly. Not having the heart to disappoint them, he gives an elaborate account of what happened: In the spring of 1958, a young man did drop in on his mother (it's highly unlikely that he came specifically for the old lady), who was 83 at that time. Her senility hindered mutual communication. She didn't recall anything valuable before passing away. Such a pity. The former Taoist priest is overcome with grief.

Others find it hard to relate to such a commonplace story. They expected something that could prove the Eaglewood Pavilion's cultural and historical significance. Fearing that he might be too worked up to watch his language, Mrs. Huang gives him a subtle warning: Focus on what his mother said, especially the outlandish tales she might have told.

Her words tingle down the former Taoist priest's spine. He glances quickly at her, picks up his handbag, and retreats into his room without a word. Mrs. Huang expected too much of him. Her language sounded like an order. No wonder the former Taoist priest was scared away …

Dawei is lying lazily in bed. He really wants to read his six or seven newspapers, but the noise outside makes it impossible to focus. His neighbors' daydreaming amuses him. He feels a strong urge to go out and throw cold water on the enthusiasm of those naive old people: If the Eaglewood Pavilion is a cultural relic, all distressed houses in the Old Town will become historical, and your bodies will all be excavated! However, in the end he doesn't speak out. Why offend your neighbors?

The event alerts the former Taoist priest: After the landing outside his door and the antique urn handed down by his ancestors, his neighbors want more from him. Determined not to be taken advantage of again, he falls back into the old routine: Go to work early, come home late, keep a stony face, no smiles, ignore all greetings. Unfortunately, this is an arduous task and his facial muscles hurt. Even worse, while the former priest climbs a foot, the "devil" climbs ten! For example, just as he is to cross the threshold of the Eaglewood Pavilion today, Caihua's bright greeting has reached his earshot, "Hello, Uncle Li, you're back home!"

Somehow, the former Taoist priest can't help but respond to the sight of her lively rosy cheeks, "Yes, I'm back." As soon as the words are out, he makes for his room, utterly flustered. Caihua was careful with her wording. "You're back home" invokes warmth and all kinds of nice human feelings. If he doesn't go away immediately, who knows what he may blurt out the next!

Caihua is well educated and conducts herself in a way appropriate to a woman whose husband is almost never home. By contrast, Mrs. Huang is not only unnatural in speech and action, but also easy to see through. For example, she shows great concern for the former Taoist priest's welfare whenever the two meet. Knowing he has to transfer twice on his commute, she tunes in to the weather forecast every night in order to warn him against possible rain the next day, or to tell him to change into warm clothes and thicker bedding if there is a cold front closing in. Thanks to his Taoist indoctrination, he has been able to resist temptation so far ... but it is really stressful to be tempted day in, day out.

If you don't believe it, put yourself in the former Taoist priest' shoes. For instance, you've just entered the house, and you hear Mrs. Huang address you, "Hi, Uncle Li, have you had supper?" or "Hi, Uncle Li, what did you have for supper? Don't save on food, save life!" You'd be a freak not to respond to such sincere greetings. That's exactly how the former Taoist feels. Consequently, when asked "Have you had supper," he would answer honestly, "Yes, I had a bite." He thinks he is being honest, but his audience seems to detect the subtext, i.e., "I have eaten, but just a bite ..." or "I ate, but I'm hungry now." See, Mrs. Huang has got it. She proffers a bowl of noodle soup or wontons with shepherd's purse.

In fact, the former Taoist priest did have supper at his factory at 4:30 p.m. before getting off work at 5 p.m., but the one-and-a-half-hour bus journey home was so exhausting that he is hungry again when he reaches the Eaglewood Pavilion. Consequently, at the sight of the delicacy in Mrs. Huang's hand, he is at once on guard and salivating. He knows very well that this is a small favor given in expectation of a much bigger return in the future, but the aroma of the food makes him reckless: What the hell! I'll just take it and not promise anything! That blue-and-white two-eared porcelain urn is enough for me to order *sanhuang* chicken at the Xiao Shaoxing Restaurant for decades. Such thoughts help him put things into perspective and accept the food. Nevertheless, he eats with a guilty look and hardly produces any noise.

After two weeks of fine dining, Mr. Li's previously darkish face glows in health. He's on much better terms with neighbors. He's even agreed to drink with Grandpa Rice Wine.

On that day, a typhoon is moving across the sea near Shanghai. Grandpa Rice Wine's nephew, who is second mate on a fishing boat, sends him a basket of seafood. Caihua spends the entire afternoon turning it into a communal feast. At dusk, Grandpa Rice Wine invites the former Taoist priest, who has taken the day off, to join them. Mr. Li has been stressed for two weeks since neighbors started to offer him free food, and the tension has been building as food quality goes up. Yet until now he has no idea what these neighbors want from him. At Grandpa Rice Wine's insistence, he accepts the invitation, determined to make them lay their cards on the table. He smooths down his collar and strides towards the dinner table as if he were Li Yuhe (a hero in the Peking opera *The Red Lantern*) approaching the feast-cum-trap set up by Hatoyama, *The Red Lantern*'s main villain.

Unlike usual guests who toast each other and play games, the former Taoist priest is very discreet. After two cups of wine, he grows ashamed of himself: His host doesn't hatch any sinister plot. Grandpa Rice Wine invited him only because he wanted him to taste the fresh catch, join in the merry-making, and have some small talk.

The thing about small talk is that you never know where the conversation will go. As they wine and dine, neighbors somehow pick up the usual topics: Caihua complains about housing; Mrs. Huang laments the her son's ill luck; Grandpa Rice Wine talks over past and present, ending up with the famous Small Swords general nicknamed "Little Mirror" ...

Mr. Li turns a deaf ear to them. Eyes contemplating the nose, nose contemplating the heart, he makes as if doing some religious breathing exercise, but in fact he is missing his faraway son. How he wants to drown his sorrows in wine! After three or four drinks, he feels like speaking. Should he speak, he asks himself? Why not? Seize the moment! He bangs his cup onto the table and fires away.

"Old Tippler. We've drunk enough. Why don't you speak your mind?" He eyes the others defiantly. Drinking indeed emboldens people. Some onlookers believe that even if he knew a public denouncement rally is the next on the agenda, he would have spoken the following, "If you treat me in good faith, you must not expect me to treat you back. I can't afford it. If you have other plans, the wine today is hardly enough for me alone!"

"There is more wine. Here, take these …" Grandpa Rice Wine is half drunk. With trembling hands, he fishes out two bottles of Tung Hua Wine from under the table, which were to be given to the second mate as gift in return.

"Good!" The former Taoist priest gives vent to his pent-up indignation. "Come on! Tell me what you want from me. Is it antique, land, or my life?" He stands up abruptly, his blood-shot eyes glaring. It wouldn't be surprising at all if he overturned the table and did a Taoist sword dance the next minute!

"Li Rihai! Uncle Li! Linglong's dad!" Mrs. Huang mind works all the better in an emergency. She calls him "Linglong's dad," a term he hasn't heard for years. He is mollified. She steps quickly forward to massage his bony shoulder blades while speaking in a soothing voice, "Look at you. Getting paranoid again! The bad times were over … Oh, about your urn. It all comes back to me. Xiaomao! Xiaomao!" She shouts at the top of her lung although she knows very well her son is out on a date, "Damn kid! He lent it to someone else. Who is it? Oh yes, a fellow worker with a runny nose. That guy keeps goldfish in it. Xiaomao even gave him two Bubble Eyes."

Mrs. Huang rarely apologizes. The former Taoist priest is unnerved. He wonders whether he has gone too far.

Other neighbors take the opportunity to further pacify him. The former Taoist priest doesn't relent until Baobao makes a childish request, "Grandpa Priest, can you tell me a story?"

"A story? Do you want me to tell you a story?! Very well …" he bends down to gather Baobao into his arms. Old people like children. Baobao is a naughty boy. He often peeps in when the old man is taking a bath in summer, or throws firecrackers into his room upon festivals to scare him. But the old man likes him anyway. In normal circumstances, the former Taoist priest would have a grandson of his own. "What story do you want to hear?"

"About the ... Small Swords Association!"

"Small Swords Association? All right. My mother used to tell me about it when I was little ..." the former Taoist priest narrows his eyes into slist, rests his head on Baobao's shoulder, and reminisces under the influence of the wine ...

What a titillating reminiscence it is! Gibberish aside, the main idea is: The Small Swords Association general nicknamed "Little Mirror" did once stay at the Eaglewood Pavilion, and the much renowned Liu Lichuan did visit the Eaglewood Pavilion.

This is major. Grandpa Rice Wine sobers up at once. Mouth agape, liver-colored nose in sharp contrast with pale lips, he stares at the former Taoist priest. Mrs. Huang falls all over herself to offer the latter more wine.

"Have some wine. Drink up!" The former Taoist priest takes a swig, slams down the wine cup, waves his arm, and glowers.

"Don't you believe me? Fine. Follow me. I'll show you." He staggers out. Others are frightened.

"Uncle Li, sit down."

"Sit down. Let's keep drinking!"

The former Taoist priest shoves them aside looking thoroughly ferocious. He slurs as he stumbles out of the room, "Sword? Sword! Sword ..." There is a commotion in the house comparable to the one when the Japanese invaders charged into a refugee camp. Mrs. Huang wants to bite her tongue off—she shouldn't have flattered this diabolical priest just to facilitate her son's marriage. What if the old man takes class revenge by the excuse of intoxication? This is life-and-death matter! Luckily, Caihua hasn't lost her mind. She steps forward to support the former Taoist priest with her hand, addressing him as "Uncle Li" or "Linglong's dad" repeatedly. Such intimacy turns out to be quite effective. The former Taoist priest loses his murderous look immediately.

"Caihua, I can walk on my own. Sword, small sword, I'm going to show you ..."

Chairs and stools clatter to the floor. Who doesn't want to have a sneak preview of the said cultural relic!

The former Taoist priest rummages out a rusty knife from the bottom of a chest. It looks like a wood chopper or a dagger, but no one is sure until Dawei, who arrives late on the scene and fearing a murder has taken place, inspects it closely and declares it to be just a knife for peeling sugar canes. The scorn on his face nettles the former Taoist priest. He grabs Dawei, who is naked except for a pair of drawers, and forces the latter to have a closer look at some indistinguishable engraving on the back of the knife blade. Dawei obliges, but he can't make it out. At the same time he still thinks it possible that Mr. Li used it to peel sugar canes when he was out of regular employment.

Leaving his daydreaming neighbors in the dim lamplight, Dawei crawls dispiritedly back into bed.

"What happened?" his wife, who was buttoning her clothes impatiently, is terrified.

"Nuts!" Dawei clenches his teeth. "Go back to sleep!" He suspects the former Taoist priest was avenging himself. Sure enough, the same night, as Dawei tosses and turns in bed, he overhears Mr. Li giggle in his sleep like a girl ...

This historic night injects joy and hope into the Eaglewood Pavilion—in the foreseeable future, the Eaglewood Pavilion will get a new lease of life. However, Dawei is distressed. Why? He has become impotent since that night. He was making love to his wife when the chilling shouts about "swords" reached his ears ... such a fright! To make matters worse, cure for such a modern urban disease is hard to find! He is listless and dejected all day long.

Nothing has happened in the two weeks since the letter penned by the former Taoist priest was put into the mail. He is surprised. Grandpa Rice Wine is impatient. Caihua is discouraged.

"Who mailed it?" Dawei asks stiffly, as if he were to pick a fight with someone the next minute. The painful experience has taught him a lesson: He will regain his masculinity only when this damned house is identified as a historic site!

Who mailed it? It goes without saying. The former Taoist priest wrote the letter, Caihua contributed the envelope, Grandpa Rice Wine sealed it, and it fell on Mrs. Huang to put it into the mail. Dawei secretly doubts whether she paid adequate postage, but he doesn't speak out. Otherwise, the old lady will be infuriated. The root cause is eventually attributed to the former Taoist priest who, in his tipsy state that day, addressed the letter to "Leaders Concerned at Municipal Government Departments Concerned." In China, the term "concerned" is very ambiguous. God knows who is concerned with a matter and who isn't! Sometimes it takes a year or two to clarify accountability.

These days, Dawei feels a kettle boiling in his loins. He needs some way to let off steam; even a quarrel will do. When it occurs to him that seeking out the "concerned" authorities is a good diversion, he gets on his old bicycle. Before he leaves, Mrs. Huang exhorts him, "Dawei, don't leave out the horizontal inscribed board!" "Dawei, don't rush when you speak. First tell them about the sword, then ..." "Dawei, do you remember the uncle who ran a tofu stall ..." To tell the truth, Dawei knows very well what he should do: Talk eloquently, appeal to reason as well as human compassion ... in short, he must do whatever he can to convince the authorities of the Eaglewood Pavilion's historical significance.

Off he goes to the museum, the Cultural Relics Administration, and the History Society. What follows is his speech at the History Society, "Our ancient building bore witness to the Taiping Revolution. We found several weapons used by the Small Swords Association, including a dagger that belonged to the General 'Little Mirror.' The pity is a child named Baobao sold it for some pear syrup. There is also a horizontal board inscribed with 'Residence of General Sky-high.' Mrs. Huang, a shrewd woman in our building, uses it as a floor joist. Comrades, if we don't act now, these precious cultural relics will be destroyed! We'll let our ancestors down, deprive our offspring of the memory of the past, and disrupt history! I'd like to reiterate: I know the world is rife with bureaucracy and national nihilism, but I'll do what I can to speak out to the world, the entire country, and the general public: Preserve history, preserve the Eaglewood Pavilion, and preserve our conscience."

His speech moves a tottering old gentleman with a wrinkled face, who asks him to write down the address of the Eaglewood Pavilion. Three days later, two people arrive at the house. One wears a lined, short gown with buttons down the front, and the other leans on a bamboo cane. They are exhausted after spending more than three hours looking for the Eaglewood Pavilion, which is not a good sign. Even worse, it is Mrs. Huang who answers the door. She mistakes the two ordinary-looking old men for pensioners working part-time for the Housing Administration, so she gives them a long list of defects of the house. It's not until they ask her about a horizontal inscribed board that she comes to her senses, but it is too late. She shows them the floor joist soiled by kitchen fumes.

The two old men mumble to each other, "Mm, this one with two horizontal strokes may be the character *zhuang*. That one with a vertical stroke in the middle may be the *zhong*. And is that the character *rou*?"

"I think so. Let's read the inscription from left to right, *zhuang rou tian zhong*. It doesn't make any sense. From right to left, *zhong tian rou zhuang* ..." What? This is not a board for a general's residence, but a signboard for a butcher's! The two old men look at each other, smiling and nodding. Even as obtuse as Mrs. Huang is, she knows it's bad. Then the laughter becomes louder, so loud that the entire Eaglewood Pavilion seems to tremble.

Thank God they're still interested in the sword. Mrs. Huang searches high and low. Eventually she presents to them a shabby cleaver. The two old men are amused. Mrs. Huang is deeply humiliated. With a signboard for a butcher's and a cleaver, isn't she crying up wine and selling vinegar?

"A former Taoist priest keeps the sword in his chest. Do stay for supper. When he comes back, you'll see we didn't lie ..." Mrs. Huang is sweating. Then she remembers that she hasn't even served tea! But what's the point? Even coffee won't help now!

The dilapidated house arouses the compassion of the two old gentlemen. Instead of sitting down for tea, they go around the house to check its condition, promising to urge the competent authorities to repair it before the rainy season. Upon leaving, they tell Mrs. Huang: Ask the young man to bring the engraved sword over when it is convenient. It won't take long ...

When Mrs. Huang recounts what happened to Dawei the same night, he laughs so hard that he bends down and tears well up in his eyes. Extreme joy begets sorrow. This is the best case in point. Interestingly, the emotional roller coaster energizes Dawei. That night, he is able to make love to his wife again. Afterwards, holding his wife's tiny body in his arms, he smiles to himself. Ha, Mrs. Huang urged him to send them the sword. Thank God he was not at home that afternoon, otherwise the two old men might have asked for reimbursement of their transportation expenditure and charge for the loss of half a day's working time ...

# VI

There is a discipline named "communication studies" in foreign countries. One can even obtain master's degree in it. Actually, such studies exist in China, too. Listen, Mrs. Huang is communicating another piece of news: A housing surveyor spent three hours in Mrs. Party Secretary's attic. He also drank two cups of malted milk.

"What would you expect? After all, her husband is long dead," Caihua comments with compassion. She believes Mrs.

Huang, whose north window faces Mrs. Party Secretary's "manhole." Since no one draws the curtain in broad daylight, Mrs. Huang becomes the authoritative source of information on Mrs. Party Secretary. Thanks to Mrs. Huang, Caihua is knowledgeable about her neighbors at the Eaglewood Pavilion and even the entire neighborhood. Who knows, maybe she doped the malted milk! Go on! Caihua secretly urges Mrs. Huang to say something more sensational.

To her surprise, Mrs. Huang announces, "Our house will be demolished!"

"You must be hearing voices."

"The wind blew from the south. Their voices were as clear as day!"

Caihua feels a pang of jealousy. She is putting on extra weight constantly, whereas Mrs. Party Secretary, although over forty, is still slender and speaks in a coaxing voice. No wonder men volunteer information only to women like her.

Mrs. Huang is unnerved by Caihua's silence. She is a bit afraid of the younger woman. Although they have never confronted each other directly, she is no stranger to Caihua's brawls with her father-in-law. Therefore she fawns on her, "Let's ask around and get ready. Things nowadays change so quickly."

"Who can I ask?" Caihua's voice is curt. "I can't just drag a man into my room and shut the door."

"Caihua," Mrs. Huang smiles slyly, "if you don't mind, let your father-in-law ..."

"Why should I mind? The old man drinks at two meals out of three. As long as she is willing to ... ha, ha." Caihua laughs aloud, happy to have a way to get even with Mrs. Party Secretary.

Mrs. Party Secretary considers her neighbors at the Eaglewood Pavilion beneath her attention, except for the Dings and Grandpa Rice Wine. The reasons she gets along with each of them differ. She treats the Dings as friends because Dawei is public-spirited, kind, and unaffected, while Mrs. Tian is well educated, gentle, and quiet. By contrast, the old tippler is just a handyman. He takes message from visiting relatives and friends if she is not in. He helps her pay utility bills. Even so, she appreciates his broad-mindedness. He sometimes gives her ingratiating looks right after she has fallen out with Caihua. He even whispers to her with a smell of alcohol in his breath when Caihua is not looking, "Ignore her. Her mouth is only fit to stuff her own head in!" or "Curse her! Harder!"

If Caihua catches him red-handed, she shouts orders at him. "You slacker, fill the thermal flask!" or "Take the spittoon out!" The old man follows the orders happily because it assuages his sense of guilt. This proves his broad-mindedness.

So it's settled. When Grandpa Rice Wine finishes drinking at the next meal, he is dispatched to the attic with a notebook, feigning electricity meter reading. He takes his time up there while his daughter-in-law is laden with anxiety. Mrs. Party Secretary's two kids are out. What if Grandpa Rice Wine behaves inappropriately? What if he invades her privacy? Caihua has had such experiences before. How she regrets sending this incompetent "agent" at Mrs. Huang's urging.

Grandpa Rice Wine comes down after an hour, a smile lingering on his face. His stately conduct is unusual. What is it? She eyes him. She can't speak out because the floorboard is too thin to prevent voices from travelling. Grandpa Rice Wine ignores her. He settles against the made-up bedding and dozes off. Knowing him well, Caihua can tell he has gotten something major. In usual times she would rouse him and make him tell, but this is no usual time. Give him a break. Otherwise, his booming voice ...

Tok tok tok. Mrs. Party Secretary has put on her high heels, which means she is ready to go out. In a moment, the wooden stairs creak, a wave of indescribably sweet perfume drifts in the passageway, and the pretty figure of a woman materializes outside the Eaglewood Pavilion. Caihua loses no time gazing at the receding figure. She hastens to shake the snoring Grandpa Rice Wine awake. The latter was strolling in the Grand Void until Caihua dragged him back to this world. Annoyed, he bellows, "Gross!" Caihua shows disgust at his highhandedness.

She points a finger toward the ceiling. "What did that woman tell you?"

"The entire neighborhood will be pulled down to make room for high-rises like the Park Hotel!"

"What!" For a moment Caihua can't see anything. She lands staggeringly on the edge of the bed like a shot-down fighter plane. This piece of news has come out of the blue. It's so exciting! She has been ailing all over during the long years waiting for it to come! She will soon move into a high-rise with elevators and air-conditioning. Sorrow overcomes her. She buries her face in her hands, crying.

Caihua is so sentimental. Although Grandpa Rice Wine sees no point in crying, he likes the way his daughter-in-law looks. With tears streaming down her face, she is not ferocious at all. Caihua would cry to her heart's content if Mrs. Huang didn't descend on them.

"Everything will be pulled down!" Mrs. Huang lowers her voice, her face beaming. Apparently, she has kept both Grandpa Rice Wine and Mrs. Party Secretary under surveillance. "The government is determined to push aside all obstacles and difficulties and demolish rundown houses." In her excitement she alters a once-famous quotation from Chairman Mao.

"Our new mayor comes from the construction industry. Of course he is interested in new buildings."

"Exactly. A boxer never spends a day without practicing boxing, and a singer never passes a day without practicing singing!"

... Other people chime in.

The Eaglewood Pavilion is once again bustling with discussion. For a few days, the topic never deviates from housing, just as stars never break their orbits around the sun.

Dawei keeps his cool. It's still embarrassing to recall how he inspired and then crushed the hope of his neighbors last time. He isn't going to make the mistake again; neither does he wish others to repeat it. So he just smiles when the topic comes up. However, he intends the smile to be sardonic, because he really doesn't want people to make fools of themselves again.

After supper, Dawei lies down in bed, hoping to get some sleep before his night shift, but the neighbors are just too loud. So he drapes a jacket over himself, holds its front together with both hands, goes into the passageway, and tries to dampen their enthusiasm with his sardonic smile. They turn a blind eye to him. At his wit's end, he ventures, "Quiet. Let me tell you a story!" A story? How extraordinary! They stare at him in bewilderment. He proceeds to tell the story listlessly. It is a very boring story. What follows is the gist of it:

One winter night, two beggars who hung out together found accommodation in a crumbling temple. They sat on the floor back-to-back to stay warm. The older beggar dozed off and his body slid sideways. He stretched out an arm to support himself. His hand felt a copper coin on the floor. The younger beggar, who propped himself up with both hands, also found a cold copper coin. They chatted to kill the long night. The older beggar asked the younger one, "What would you do if you had money?" The younger one answered, "I'd buy chicken." The older beggar said, "It doesn't pay to buy chicken. I'd buy eggs. Then I'd hatch chickens. With chickens there will be more eggs. And it would go on and on." The younger beggar disagreed, "Without the first chicken, how can you hatch more chickens?" They ended up in a fistfight. *Yamen* (government office in feudal China) runners arrested them for the government officer to interrogate. The officer banged his gavel, "Where did you get the copper coins?" The two beggars replied in unison, "We picked them up from the floor." The officer ordered, "Show me!" They took out the copper coins. Damn! They were two thin carrot slices …

It's a dull story, and people fail to get the undertone. They think Dawei just wanted to humor them in order to have some undisturbed sleep. Sensitive and sensible as they are, they break up dispiritedly.

Dawei's carrot slices seem to have sobered Grandpa Rice Wine up. Instead of sipping at his wine, he just stares blankly at the crystal clear wine glass. Are the carrot slices to hard to chew? No. He doesn't comprehend the story; neither will he bother pondering it. He is missing his "faraway" daughter. Back when his daughter was a budding beauty, there were many suitors. After careful screening, she locked her eyes on a baby-faced young man. The pity was the young man lived in an overcrowded dwelling. Grandpa Rice Wine refused to give his blessing. The girl vowed in a pique to marry someone with a big house. Her wish eventually came true, but the house was far away in a place named Zhujiajiao on the outskirts of Shanghai. When she went away to live in Zhujiajiao, there were tears in her eyes. Grandpa Rice Wine felt as though a knife had been plunged into his heart. To this day, any lucent liquid would remind him of his daughter's teary eyes … he owes her. It's time to pay up.

"Caihua." There is affection in Grandpa Rice Wine's voice. "I plan to go out tomorrow."

Caihua looks up from her rice bowl. The old man sounds weird, but he shouldn't have lost his mind already because his wine glass is still four-fifths full. "Where to?"

"The countryside."

"Ningbo? Do you want to sell our ancestral home?" She arches her eyebrows.

"No way! I'm going to Qingpu, to Zhujiajiao!"

"Why?" Caihua is even more alarmed. Does the old man want to gripe about her to her sister-in-law? That woman has an even more fiery temper than she does. Grandpa Rice Wine clears his throat contemptuously. Then he whispers an explanation. Caihua is befuddled: What does he want? Rename his daughter's son as his legal heir?! She bangs down her bowl in protest. Grandpa Rice Wine gives further explanation. All her suspicion is dispelled. The old man wants to change his daughter's permanent residence back here so that they will be allocated a bigger apartment during redevelopment. It's for the sake of her and Baobao.

Grandpa Rice Wine finishes his wine quickly. He goes to bed without watching the live broadcast soccer game he longed so much for. He is proud of his quick wit. Alas, how wrong he is. There are people more driven than him. Just listen to the noise upstairs.

Who makes the noise? Xiaomao. He decided to replace the three beams last night. These are solid ash beams with diameters as large as that of a large bowl. Timber rationed out by the government is of a much lower quality. He can make a wardrobe out of them, plus a nightstand, probably.

Xiaomao is known far and wide for his action orientation. He may be irresolute when courting girls, but he acts without delay over any other matter. "If you remove the beams, the entire house will come down!" His mother is concerned.

"It's going to come down anyway. I'm saving our government some man-hours!" replies Xiaomao cheerfully.

Dawei and his wife suffer greatly these days. Their neighbors seem to be possessed by the carrot slices. Dawei loses his appetite and sleeps badly. Tian Xiaoyuan loses her sanguinity, too. She fears that Dawei may get injured at work because he doesn't rest well. That night, the noise Xiaomao made as he removed the beams kept Dawei wide awake. Thank God he was tough enough to survive the next eight-hour night shift. Once home, he hit the sack without eating or drinking. He slept as if in shock and didn't wake up the next day, which is his day off.

Tian Xiaoyuan is so scared that she almost calls for an ambulance. Others' opinions vary as to why Dawei sleeps so long. Some think he does it on purpose, while others believe his vitality has dwindled. Dawei doesn't care what they think, as long as it shuts them up and allows him to sleep well. This turns out to be wishful thinking. A few nights later, he is awakened by a shrill, "Help!" His wife makes to get up. Strength before beauty. He leaps out of bed and shields his tiny wife.

He pulls the door open gingerly. The moonlight is faint.

All is dark in the passageway. His eyes gradually make out a bench that lies across the passageway. The former Taoist priest is astride it.

What is he doing? Did he just cry out for help? One question after another crosses Dawei's mind. This is unprecedented!

"Uncle Li, what, what are you doing?"

There are actually two pale patches in the dim passageway. The former Taoist priest suddenly stands up, holds his chin up, and speaks in an exceptionally clear voice, "Look at this. Isn't it taking advantage of neighbors? Isn't this bullying? Isn't it reaching out for a yard after getting an inch?"

"Stay put. No talking, no moving!" A fiercer voice erupts from a lower position in the darkness. Dawei, who is a bit near-sighted, is startled. He plucks up his courage to have a closer look at the crouching dark figure. With the shrill voice ringing in the air, the dark figure rises slowly and Dawei recognizes the lanky figure of Mrs. Huang. She is holding a hammer.

"It's you. What are you doing?" Dumbfounded, Dawei gets goose bumps.

"Dawei, still up?" Mrs. Huang greets him smilingly.

Dawei is even more baffled. "I tried to sleep. The woodpecker in your room kept me awake the other night. I thought I could sleep well tonight. But you … God!" Dawei frowns and sighs, "What was wrong?"

"He's gone nuts!" Mrs. Huang flares up. "This geezer came out with a bench, crying for help in the middle of the night. Isn't he crazy?"

"What's in your hand?!" The former Taoist priest sounds and looks fierce. His loud, clear voice pierces the still-chilly night air. "Tell us, what is it? Is it a slice, a chopstick, or a needle? Why are you holding a hammer so late in the night? Do you want to commit a murder or a robbery?"

"Slander!" Something drops to the floor. Mrs. Huang is panic-stricken. Sneaking around with a murderous weapon in hand at night, she does look like a burglar. How is she going to convince them otherwise? Grief overcomes her. How is it that she, after living in the neighborhood for fifty-six years with an unsoiled reputation, gets caught as a thief? She wants very much to look into Dawei's glaring eyes and explain: There is no evil intended. I just want to expand our "territory" in the shared kitchen … for the sake of Xiaomao. Poor Xiaomao! Maternal love emboldens her.

She speaks with righteous indignation, "Uncle Li, for a man as grown-up as you are, you should have more sympathy for others. Humanitarianism isn't just lip service …"

As the old saying goes, a good man is also a stubborn man. The former Taoist priest is indeed a kindhearted person, thanks to his upbringing and religious background. However, somehow he has no sympathy for Mrs. Huang at the moment. Instead he is in a towering rage. "Don't you try to get away with it. Stop reminding me of my past. I was a Taoist priest and I did things to harm people, but now I'm a Model Worker every year! Open your eyes and have a good look at me. Who do you think I am now?"

"Who are you now? Model Worker. Conceited Hero." Mrs. Huang speaks deliberately and coldly, "Let me tell you this, people will never forget what you did, and the eyes of the masses are always discerning."

The former Taoist priest is choked. He retorts, "Don't make insinuations. What did I do? "

…

A tug of war between a famous shrewd woman and an obstinate widower thus begins. This is a fierce battle. The past is dug up. Dawei is stuck. When can he get out? He is hoarse after all the mediation. At last he has had enough, "Drop it, both of you. And listen to me. You—" He points a finger at the former Taoist priest. "Advanced in years, no proper nutrition, long bus commute. And you," he points at Mrs. Huang, "worrying about Xiaomao all your life. What a model mother! Getting up early to stand in the front of the queue for fresh produce. Therefore, I sympathize with you both. I don't want to have kids, and my housing will only be better ..." He slows down to get it across to the dumbfounded elders. "The other day, my wife and I decided to divide our apartment into two. One half is for you—" he glances sideways at Mrs. Huang, "so for now, don't have your eyes on Uncle Li. Save your energy for Xiaomao's wedding."

Hm, you think I'm a fool, don't you? Mrs. Huang doesn't get it. "What do you mean?"

"Please," Dawei cuts her off, "feel free to have half of our apartment, please. Otherwise Uncle Li will keep getting up in the middle of the night. It's too much. To be honest," he turns to look at his own closed door briefly, looking subdued, "the day before yesterday, I was sleepy at work. I almost bumped into a locomotive ... gosh, sleep deprivation kills!"

Mrs. Huang can't tell whether Dawei has just improvised or not. She opens her mouth and shuts it again because Dawei looks troubled enough. However, the former Taoist priest is not touched by Dawei at all. Maybe his anger has been suppressed for too long, or maybe he believes Dawei is on his side. Either way, he becomes more aggressive.

"Time has passed and circumstances have changed. You can't take things away any more." He may have never been so eloquent and so rebellious in his entire life. Mrs. Huang's retort is blocked by Dawei's impartial loud voice.

"OK, OK. Stop arguing, will you both? I just don't get it. You don't take any tonic. You eat rice soaked in boiling water everyday. Where do you get all this internal heat?" He yawns expansively. "Go back to sleep. I've got a morning shift!"

The former Taoist priest is smart enough to know when to stop. He respects Dawei, anyway. On the other hand, Mrs. Huang is annoyed by Dawei's highhanded intervention, but Dawei is too popular with others at the Eaglewood Pavilion to make an enemy of. So she holds back her anger.

This turns out to be an eventful night. Dawei has barely fallen asleep when someone rustles outside. Who is it this time? Is it a burglar? Xiaomao's stereo receiver with four speakers and dual tracks is at risk ... he slips on his shoes, moves quietly behind the door, where he gropes for an extra-large wrench—now he is ready for attack. He unlatches the door and opens it slightly. A strong beam of light blinds him temporarily. What's going on? Caihua's door is wide open and her room is brightly lit. He rubs his eyes and collects himself. What! Grandpa Rice Wine is piling up some old bricks passed to him by Caihua into a wall in the passageway. The "Great Wall" has already gone up quite a bit.

It takes Dawei a long while to comprehend what is happening before his eyes: Grandpa Rice Wine and Caihua also want to expand their floor area secretly. What Dawei doesn't know is that Grandpa Rice Wine came back from Zhujiajiao empty-handed. His daughter refused to send her only son to live with them because Caihua is such a shrewd woman ...

Dawei closes the door carefully and gropes his way back to bed. Well, what can he say? They are tampering with the space outside their door. Why play a busybody ... one day he will make all this public. By and by, he drifts off. "Ouch!" someone cries out painfully. Dawei almost jumps. He pricks up his ears. Someone is moaning? Who is it? It's a person speaking with a Suzhou accent? Mrs. Party Secretary. Is she having a stomachache or ... he checks the luminous watch on his wrist. Oh yes, it is Mrs. Party Secretary on her way to the early morning shift at the restaurant. She bumped into the "Great Wall" that had appeared miraculously overnight. Sure enough, a door creaks open and Caihua's voice is heard, "Oh, I'm so sorry. Where were you hurt?" She sounds soft and apologetic. "The damned wall popped out of the blue ... I'm OK." Mrs. Party Secretary is reasonably polite. This is their first conversation after the lengthy cold war between the two. A lump comes into Dawei's throat.

The Eaglewood Pavilion quiets down again. Dawei can't sleep. He has himself worked up and wants to curse, "You shameless people! Do you want to drag everybody else down?" However, the sight of his sound-asleep wife changes his mind. He lies there, gasping.

The next day, Dawei's patience goes out. He drags himself back home at dusk, pulling a long face. He doesn't greet anyone— he used to laugh and joke with others. When Baobao begs him for a bike ride, he pretends not to hear. What can he say to these neighbors?

He pushes his bike into the passageway and stops dead. All kinds of barricades have been erected. There is no room for his bike! Anger starts to burn in his heart ...

Others misinterpret Dawei's hesitation as regret. Embarrassed, the early birds want to make up with him. Caihua offers him part of her "territory." Mrs. Huang follows suit. And then all others second the motion. If they kept quiet, Dawei would feel better— at least silence indicates shame. But instead of feeling ashamed, they try to drag him down. Anger bursts out:

"Thank you. Thank you so much!" Dawei locks the bike vehemently. "Such space is not worthy of my attention. If I wanted to do it, I'd do it grander. I'd take up the whole passageway, or a street, or all of Shanghai ... then, I'll kick out all these calculating, scheming, and noisy people!" He heads for his room, leaving the neighbors looking at each other ...

# VII

Hope is like a shooting star. It comes and goes in the blink of an eye. The messy passageway becomes even messier. No wonder Dawei keeps telling the tale of two carrot slices. If he had put two actual carrot slices into a bowl every time he told the story, he would have had enough to make a salad by now.

Redevelopment rolls out in Lane 96 across from the Eaglewood Pavilion.

The silence of the Eaglewood Pavilion's residents is palpable. If any insensitive person makes any insensitive comment at a time like this, he will very likely bear the brunt of their anger. Nevertheless, the rumble of the pile drivers across the street rocks them to and fro. Anyone who has flown knows that when a plane rocks in turbulence, the best thing to do is to open the mouth.

"The earth is trembling. I just hope that everything across the street collapses!"

"Collapse is nothing. Tangshan Earthquake buried all people alive!"

"I wish I were buried alive. Much better than I am now!"

"Don't lose heart. A single spark can start a prairie fire."

"It's all about luck!" Mrs. Huang can hardly contain herself. She planned to wash rice before cooking, but she forgot. Luckily, unwashed rice still smells fragrant when cooked. Also, it's said that washing causes vitamin loss, and vitamin deficiency causes athlete's foot. "Look at the state of this house. I thought they would knock down ours first ... but those go first! Who made the decision? Are they blind?"

"The houses over there? Of course they go first." Grandpa Rice Wine comments knowingly, "Who are we in this house, and who lives over there?!" He pauses for dramatic effect. When others are drawn to him, he lets the bomb drop, "Do you remember the old woman from Wenzhou who practiced *qigong* at the entrance to Lane 96 every day? The woman with a plaster stuck to her temple to get rid of a headache? Her son is our district magistrate!"

"Forget that old lady! I think it's because of the mangy fruit seller on our street. His father works at the Housing Administration." Mrs. Huang is not resigned to play second fiddle. "He used to go to school with Xiaomao. Later he went to work in a rural production team in Northern Jiangsu. Then he got sick, came back to Shanghai, and set up the fruit stall ... Xiaomao's classmate. Of course I know."

"OK. Let's just say it's because of his father." Grandpa Rice Wine is impatient with Mrs. Huang's obsession with details. "Anyway, to make a long story short, they have pull, they've got connections! What do we have? Nothing." He shrugs like a foreigner and shakes his head.

On that day, Dawei feels exceptionally refreshed after a good sleep following his night shift. He is pacing inside his room, hands on his back. As he listens to his neighbors on the other side of the thin wall, refutation dances up and down inside him, shouting, "Let me out!" But considering the strained relationship with his neighbors recently, he thinks better of it and remains quiet. However, Grandpa Rice Wine has gone too far with the "connections." He paces out.

"Grandpa Rice Wine. In my mind," he says, trying to be affable, "this is not about connections. People in Lane 96 were relocated because they have the big picture. They are not engrossed in personal gains and losses ..."

Dawei's politically correct comment dampens the others' spirits. Some may harbor unspoken criticism, "Who are you to lecture us?" But then, on second thought, they think Dawei was right. Look at the passageway. There is not even room left for his bicycle ...

Grandpa Rice Wine doesn't take Dawei's mild criticism well. He gulps his wine instead of taking sips, as if he were taking out his anger at the wine. Afterward, he goes directly to bed. No TV program can distract him. By contrast, Mrs. Huang is not depressed at all. In her opinion, Dawei's comments were far from profound. After seeing the well-groomed Xiaomao off, she heads for the construction site across the street with mixed feelings.

The whistling and rumbling of construction machinery across the street has been a torture for residents of the Eaglewood Pavilion these days. Some try to live with it. Others tackle it. For example, Mrs. Huang "combats poison by poison": She does "standing exercise" at the construction site. In a fortnight she has been there at least a dozen times. She always rests her chin on a sparse bamboo fence and stands still for three-quarters of an hour. Sometimes she falls into a trance and talks to herself. If there is a listener—acquaintance and stranger alike—she gives them an earful: Xiaomao's misfortune; the scoop on why Lane 96 was redeveloped ahead of the Eaglewood Pavilion; the grave consequence of evil social practices. The standing exercise may have blocked blood circulation, because when she walks home afterward, she drags her feet and her shoes scrape the ground.

The scraping gets on others' nerves. Caihua can't take this any more. She tries to bring Mrs. Huang to her senses. "Why are you so keen on it? What's the point? I'd rather keep it out of sight!"

Caihua's coping mechanism is indeed more positive than Mrs. Huang's. Every evening, after supper, she finds diversion in attending local opera performances. On her way out, she always makes a detour to stay clear of the construction sites. This is how she explains it, "I don't fancy it at all. Out of sight, out of mind."

Grandpa Rice Wine considers himself above both Mrs. Huang and his daughter-in-law. In his opinion, the former has lost her mind while the latter has become a fool—throwing money into the Huangpu River for some damned singing and dancing (since they had TV at home, he has been comparing theater-going to "throwing money into the Huangpu River"). In order to cancel out the noise from across the street, he turns up the volume of the TV set to maximum. After only two days, the speakers of the TV set break down. It's no fun reading lips. Later, Caihua stays in after supper: She has watched *Five Daughters Celebrating Father's Birthday* six times. Moreover, she comes to think it unwise to defy something by spending money. Stuck at home with only each other as company, Grandpa Rice Wine and his daughter-in-law develop a routine of verbal abuses before bedtime every night. They find a way to vent their anger, while their neighbors get entertained. Killing two birds with one stone, how economical! Listen, here they go again:

"The rumbling is driving me crazy!"

"Stop whining. I have a morning shift!"

"Are you deaf? Who can sleep with the noise? Not unless you have a soundproof room!"

"You don't have such good fortune. That old woman with back-door connections has!"

"Damn good fortune! I just don't want to kiss asses. If I do, I will open all doors, front doors, back doors, emergency exits!"

"Don't you dare. People in back-door deals get their feet caught in the door!"

"So you're the only pure soul left on earth. Without the back door you can't even get into a crematorium ..."

"Wait and see. The government should launch a movement against people using back doors!"

"Exactly. This is too much. State secrets, economic intelligence and redevelopment plans have all leaked out through back doors ..."

So it goes on and on. This is the way Caihua and her father-in-law work off their anger. They have no idea whether Mrs. Party Secretary has fallen asleep or not. If she hasn't, it's impossible for her not to hear the two-person show one thin floor below. She should have stormed down and demanded apologies. Actually, Mrs. Party Secretary hears it all. She is indignant at first: Hm, a movement against me, break my feet ... but then the sleeping pill happens to take effect. She drops off ...

This has been an unusual time period in the history of the Eaglewood Pavilion. All TV sets and radio-cassette recorders seem to have shorted out. A heavy stillness shrouds the house as soon as night falls. Dawei enjoys the rare silence with heart and soul. He doesn't show it in public, though. On the other hand, he feels the silence is a bit gloomy, a bit chilly, and a bit lifeless. So he examines his attitude towards neighbors: Has he been too harsh on them?

At nightfall, as Dawei shuts himself up and ponders his mistakes, there is a knock on the door. He opens it and—surprise! It is a smiling, well-dressed Mrs. Party Secretary. With her wafts the scent of violets. This is unusual, and it is already an unusual time. Dawei tells her Ms. Tian is holding a parents' meeting at school. Mrs. Party Secretary doesn't mind. Dawei invites her in awkwardly. Mrs. Party Secretary explains with a soft Suzhou accent, "Bingbing is graduating from primary school this year. He plans to apply to a top middle school and would therefore like to get some guidance from Ms. Tian." She produces

Bingbing's composition book for Ms. Tian to look over in her spare time. In return for this favor, she mentions in passing, "The redevelopment plan has been finalized. This neighborhood will be demolished in the near future. The source is credible. Get prepared. Don't tell others ..."

Mrs. Party Secretary's warning against telling others is superfluous. People like Dawei and Ms. Tian are not gossips. Dawei likes the part about getting prepared much better. "Get ready." These two magic words lift his spirits at once: Yes, this is what he has been looking forward to. That night, Dawei has sex without protection. It's an occasion of joy and longing. It's also time to crush rumors about their infertility ... humankind is self-interested, after all!

Xiaomao decides to go back to school. Political upheavals disrupted his years of former education. It's better for a bachelor to spend his free time studying than loafing around. Mrs. Huang doesn't think so. Knowing her son, she worries that Xiaomao may have grown disillusioned and considered becoming a monk. There is little hope for their house to be pulled down soon, let alone redeveloped. Without new housing, no girl will marry him. Without a wife, there is no difference from being a monk. Standing at 178 centimeters and well over thirty years old, he has nowhere to go in the evenings because the streets are teeming with couples. How sad!

Mrs. Huang is distressed at her son's plan to go back to school. Xiaomao has forgotten most of what he learned in his few years of formal education. He is not known for being smart. Moreover, he talks in his sleep. If he sets high goals for himself this time, he may get overworked. This topic is inserted into Mrs. Huang's speech during her "standing exercise." She is flaunting a bit—of course she has no idea that her son is to go back to school to study things he should have been taught at primary and secondary schools—in China, nothing is loftier than education.

While Mrs. Huang considers Xiaomao's going back to school

as a kind of voluntary celibacy, Xiaomao has his own reasons. His lonely-heart ad has appeared three times in the newspaper. It was with trepidation that he lied about his looks, stylizing himself as "handsome" or "boasting classic features."

What felt even worse was asking his employer to provide a reference to the newspaper. They started to make fun of him: "Whee, Xiaomao, still sifting sand for gold? Listen to this old man. Don't raise the bar. Lower it." Or, "Well, a reference for you again? What happened to the last one? You lost it? Cut it out. I saw your ad in the overseas edition of the *People's Daily* ..."

To hell with lonely-heart ads. He then tried dating agencies. They didn't require references, but they arranged ballroom dances. Unmarried men and women in their thirties or older had to hold hands like preschoolers. It was cute, but it also felt weird. To make matters worse, one must know how to "circulate" on the dance floor, and he had no knack for it at all. His sense of humor only surfaces during dreams.

Once at a ball, he accepted a woman's invitation to dance. She had an easy manner, while he was clumsy. She frowned and grimaced. What was wrong? Was she having a stomachache, or ...? She told him at his insistence that he had been stamping on her frostbitten feet. He apologized profusely. She said it was all right, but her next remark was not polite at all, "How come you dance like an Australian aboriginal?" Once home, he hurried to dance in front of the dressing mirror. Gosh, the guy in the mirror was doing martial arts. This revelation made his resist dating agencies.

Next, he decided to try his luck at a night school. It was said that many students went to adult schools to look for their Mr. or Mrs. Right, and most succeeded. "Dating your classmate" has become a fad.

Xiaomao took up with a woman at the night school, who, like him, is well above the average age for marriage, owing to housing difficulties. One night in class, Xiaomao heard a heavy sigh from the back row when the teacher explained "population density." He turned to have a look. There was a woman sitting by herself. Xiaomao took the sigh as a hint. The following night, he arrived early and took the seat beside the girl, with a plan in mind. Subsequently, the worldwide challenge of housing difficulty caused by increasing population density brought the two together.

Mrs. Huang is naturally happy for Xiaomao. In the ordinary course of events, she should be all smiles, but no, she looks morose. Why? She received word from that future daughter-in-law—the latter is coming to congratulate them on the imminent redevelopment. What? The project is getting nowhere, and there is nothing worthy of congratulation. This is tricky. Well, it was Xiaomao's fault. He gave the girl the wrong impression that redevelopment would kick off soon after Lane 96.

"How soon?" asked the girl.

"Very soon. In two to three weeks, a month the latest!" he seemed to know what he was talking about. It has been two months since his assertion. Surely resettlement is on the horizon, right?! That's why the girl wanted to see it with her own eyes. Can you blame her? Her inference is totally legitimate. On the other hand, she inferred too much from Xiaomao's vision. Had she looked into his eyes, she would have detected evasion. Nevertheless, it is not to say that Xiaomao was immoral. He made such a claim out of desperation. Without it, what girl would be interested in him?

This is urgent. Mrs. Huang can't sleep. After tossing and turning in bed, she slips on her shoes, goes downstairs noisily, sits in front of the house gate under the clear moon and few stars, and gazes at the brightly lit construction site across the street ... this way she feels easier in mind.

One night, Grandpa Rice Wine went out to use the public toilet. He almost staggered into Mrs. Huang, who was sitting in front of the house like a door-god. He was so startled that he almost peed in his underpants.

"What, what are you doing?"

Mrs. Huang's pupils glisten like luminous pearls in the hollow sockets. She is watching the construction site intently.

"Xiaomao's mother. You ... I thought ..."

Mrs. Huang is expressionless.

"... Haven't you looked at it enough during the day?"

"I want to find out who is behind this!" Mrs. Huang finally speaks through clenched teeth.

"Who is behind this? Didn't you say it was the head of the Housing Administration? The famous Lord of Housing ..."

"Lord of Housing. Housing ... I'm ... I'm going to ..." Mrs. Huang breathes heavily, "I'm going to expose him!" She grinds her teeth.

Mrs. Huang is serious. Two days later, a thin old lady who just can't stop talking lingers about the entrance to the Housing Administration on the Bund. She pesters the doorkeeper for a meeting with the Party Secretary. The doorkeeper asks, "What for?" The old lady says she wants to blow the whistle on a guy whose son has a copper coin-sized favus on the scalp. This guy is engaged in under-the-table dealings. The doorkeeper asks, "Where does he work?" The old lady replies, "At the Housing Administration." He asks, "What is his name? How old is he? Which department does he work in?" She replies, "I don't know."

The doorkeeper tells her, "It's tough to identify a person just by a scar on the scalp of his son. We do keep rather comprehensive personal dossiers, but we haven't gone as far as to make note of birthmarks, scars or favus." He asks her to come back with more specifics. The old lady refuses to go. She accuses him of bureaucratism. The doorkeeper is miffed. Firstly, he is just a small potato, not a bureaucrat. Moreover, the suffix "-ism" is reserved only for things sacred. The old lady thinks this is a typical case of bureaucrats shielding each other. She is not to be dissuaded. The doorkeeper turns to look the other way. Fine, feel free to stand there. The mantra in the 1980s is civic virtues. Passers-by try to talk her into her senses. She turns a deaf ear. Then, people start to wander if she suffers from senile dementia. After three days,

Mrs. Huang loses hope and never returns. Lucky for her, because the doorkeeper considers asking the police for help to send her to a hospital.

Mrs. Huang grows testier after her trips to the Bund. Indignation keeps her awake. She sits sighing at the house gate night after night. Her posture resembles a monk in meditation. Monks practice meditation in search for enlightenment. Enlightenment occurs to Mrs. Huang on the night when a FAW truck speeds along the pitch-dark street. After a honk, the truck reverses, and a truckload of timber is dumped noisily on the deserted construction site. After the truck leaves, Mrs. Huang spots several planks peeking out of the bamboo fence. She is drawn to them. Is it to give vent to her anger or to look for petty gains? Actually, it remains inexplicable to Mrs. Huang herself. She just feels driven to go ahead under the cover of the night and pull as hard as she can. Man, it is addictive. She goes back three nights in a row. The planks she has hoarded should be enough for a cupboard. However, on the fourth night, as she is pulling at a plank while muttering under her breath, "Damned resettlement. Damned backdoor," a pair of callous hands gripped her by the arms.

"Ha-ha, I got you!" The triumphant voice sends chills down her spine. She feels as if wakened from a dream—a two-week-long nightmare. What am I doing? Such a shame! I, a dignified neighborhood cadre and a once-famous member of the Proletarian Dictatorship Taskforce, am now stealing state property! Mrs. Huang bursts out crying, "God. I didn't mean it—"

"Why did you take them home?"

"You keep me awake!"

"Does it justify stealing?"

"I, I hate …"

"Do you hate the Four Modernizations?"

"No, not at all …" Wow, the accusation escalates! Mrs. Huang wails and shivers. She used to have a glib tongue, but now her words don't even hang together. She feels herself wronged:

Honest as she is, how is it possible for her to commit theft in the middle of the night? Yet, the planks in her hand and the broom closet can't be giveaways. She is in deep trouble.

Thank God that Dawei comes to her rescue. Otherwise she would have spent the night in detention. Dawei happens to work the middle shift that night. From far away, he spots two figures tugging back and forth. He pedals harder. It is a trembling Mrs. Huang begging for mercy from a man in a cotton-padded overcoat. What a cruel scene! Who is this man? Did he assault Mrs. Huang? Indignant, he jumps off the bike, dashes forward and grabs the man by his lapel. The man moans. Something is wrong. The man sounds like he has too much phlegm. Upon close look Dawei finds him to be an old man. Slow down, look before you jump!

Mrs. Huang feels relieved, ashamed, and scared, all at the same time. She cries out her grievances. The old picket rubs his chest and presents his case. Dawei gets a rough idea of what happened before he is done. He can't help pitying Mrs. Huang. What has gotten into her head? Although he has not been on the best terms with Mrs. Huang recently, he feels obliged to help the latter out. He must downplay her "motive." What was her motive? He doesn't have a clue. Then something he read in a newspaper comes across his mind. This might be explained by psychology! Emboldened, Dawei showed the picket his work ID and invited the latter to have a talk inside. The old picket backed off, rubbing his chest. He is not going to have a "talk" with such a big guy. Dawei changes his tactics. He gives the old man an account of the teary woman's medical history in a sincere tone: dizziness, blurred vision, insomnia, and sleep walking. He also points out that noctambulism patients are not legally liable— they don't know what they are doing, and any implicit or explicit intervention by others will cause clinical exacerbation. Therefore, he asks the old man for lenience so that the patient can return to her family and neighbors safely … "If you don't believe me, ask this old comrade!"

Grandpa Rice Wine has been listening for quite some time in his drawers. He was wakened by Dawei's booming voice. Since Dawei turns the spotlight on him, he must give testimony. Interestingly, he goes a step further, "None of us here can sleep, thanks to the noise and light pollution from your site! Sleep walk is the least of our worries. I almost get schizophrenic ..." He seems to pave the way for medical indemnities.

Seeing two neighbors guaranteeing for Mrs. Huang, the picket decides to let her go. Anyway, no hardened thief would tremble like she does, and a villain doesn't wreak havoc in his own neighborhood. Moreover, the planks are only good for a chicken pen ...

Mrs. Huang falls ill right after the "medical parole." It lasts two full weeks, although nobody knows if she is truly ill or not, because she confines herself to her attic. When Caihua visits her one day, Mrs. Huang has applied plaster to both temples, her cheeks have become sallow and dry, and a weak voice has replaced the usual piping. The first idea that comes into Caihua's mind is that the old woman is making a fuss about an imaginary disease. On second thought, the illness might be real. Think what the old lady has been up to: No sleep, petitioning to the authorities, and blowing whistles on evildoers. Such an agenda may have exhausted a young man! Therefore it's lucky for her to get just "noctambulism," not schizophrenia.

However, Mrs. Huang can't afford to linger in bed after two weeks, because something happened.

The source this time is Li Rihai, the former Taoist priest. The White Cloud Temple is said to be restored and open to the public, but it won't do to have just any Taoist priest in it. People from the United Front Work Department sought Mr. Li out and offered to reinstate him. When they came to his room, he was giving it a thorough cleaning. He couldn't even offer them a seat. The "negotiation" had to take place outside in the passageway with both parties standing. When asked if he had difficulties in life, Mr. Li answered deferentially: It's not a difficulty, but a small wish—would the leaders please reopen his son's case while reinstating his priesthood? They promised to see to it immediately. In three days Mr. Li got their feedback, "Residence registration at your neighborhood has been suspended."

Mr. Li was devastated. Others were exhilarated: There is so much to do and so little time …

# VIII

Resettlement finally begins at the Eaglewood Pavilion.

Nobody else at the Eaglewood Pavilion is entitled to any preferential treatment except for the Taoist priest. After repeated rallies, everyone knows the policy by heart: Residents who are able to find interim housing may move back when new buildings are completed; residents who aren't able to find temporary housing will be allocated new apartments along the Huangpu River.

In the ordinary course of events, residents at the Eaglewood Pavilion should be gratified. The more resourceful of them should move quickly to interim housing, and the rest should move to apartments along the Huangpu River and start anew. However, things are always more easily said than done. For the Chinese, moving means getting uprooted from one's homestead and is not to be treated lightly. Since it is not to be treated lightly, one has to consider and reconsider. As a result, unexpected events crop up.

Take Caihua as example. She regretted the resettlement agreement right after signing it, because she thought it was more appropriate to be allocated two apartments instead of one—how can a daughter-in-law and father-in-law share an apartment? Comrades from the Relocation Office stuck to principles and didn't relent. More than ten rounds of negotiations later, they were still locked in a stalemate … Caihua dropped the hint at every round: Her father-in-law, who is as strong as a horse, may very likely get remarried. The official finally lost patience. He shot back: In the spirit of gender equality, why must a woman go to live in her husband's house after the wedding? Why can't a man go to live with his wife? ... What? Caihua couldn't imagine her father-in-law living with the family of his new wife. She burst out crying. The official, who was a man over forty, didn't know what to do. He cleared his throat. "Comrade Chen Caihua, let's discuss it another time." Subsequently, her case remains unsolved.

Mrs. Huang is not as vulnerable as Caihua. Her experiences in petitioning to the authorities have taught her: Tears, like fake guns, can only make paper tigers recoil. Since she got out of bed, she has been working very hard. She took out materials she had used in petitioning and pored over them together with Xiaomao. Finally she came to a conclusion: Her household was victimized by some historical events and it is high time for the injustice to be redressed. She went immediately to see the Preparatory Taskforce for Reconstruction.

At that time, the taskforce was newly assembled. Some members, who were summoned from their previous positions as machine operators, bench workers, or bookkeepers, found it very hard to follow Mrs. Huang's logic. "Madam, take a breath and slow down. Aren't you tired? We're tired just listening!" First impressions are the strongest. Mrs. Huang became a "celebrity" with them.

One day, the taskforce leader, who looked like an engineer, came to communicate policies with residents. He was seated when Mrs. Huang appeared from the other end of the street. He swiveled immediately to turn his back to her, as if she were something ominous. Mrs. Huang was not angry. She thought it was good sign. Experience had taught her: The more others abhor her, the more likely she is to get what she demands.

The course of events did run as she expected. She was given several alternatives of relocation, but she rejected them all. She was adamant: She will not relocate unless they give her two first-floor, south-facing apartments. There were several reasons for her preference for the first floor. For starters, Mr. Xu in Lane 96 died shortly after relocation to an upstairs apartment. Secondly, she hoped to keep chickens or ducks on the first-floor corridor or the open space around the apartment building.

Of course, this was the mentality of small-scale farmers. Xiaomao spoke strongly against his mother. Mrs. Huang was not to be persuaded. Xiaomao had to call in reinforcement from the Marriage Registry at the Civil Affairs Bureau. This official spoke eloquently. She explained that the third- and fourth-floor apartments had become the most sought after ones in China. She even mentioned that Prime Minister Thatcher of the United Kingdom, the role model for women all around the world, also favored living upstairs. Mrs. Huang stood her ground. The official decided to issue a "red card." She waved a red marriage certificate. "Madam, if you insist on living on the ground floor, your future daughter-in-law may want to marry 'up!'" This was a threat! Recalling the ups and downs in finding a wife for her son, Mrs. Huang conceded. Yet to her chagrin, all third- and fourth-floor apartments had already been allocated.

Mrs. Huang felt like she was suspended in midair.

Well, how about the three other households? Mrs. Party Secretary seems to have a card up her sleeve, whereas the Taoist priest and Dawei are in low spirits. Although preferential policies were extended to the son of the former, it was impossible to get a residence registration. As for Dawei, his mother died back in his hometown several months ago. Consequently, each family will only be allocated one apartment.

Dawei always tries to look on the bright side of things. He understands the difficulty facing his employer and his neighbors. The three work units are all small-scale organizations with no experience in building apartment blocks for their workers, most of whom complain about housing inadequacies. They have worked hard to raise funds and obtain all kinds of approvals, but the construction is halted because his neighbors want more. Isn't such conduct highway robbery?

Redevelopment of the Eaglewood Pavilion is grounded.

Houses around the Eaglewood Pavilion are pulled down like weeds in the field. According to the Resettlement Taskforce, they follow a policy of "implementation when conditions are right." If implementation is obstructed, conditions may deteriorate.

Eaglewood Pavilion's residents realize that they have been sidelined. In their minds, solidarity is of the greatest importance at such a critical moment. They urge each other to follow the rules of collective bargaining. No sell-out is allowed.

Dawei find the Taoist priest a bit strange these days. The latter used to demonstrate no interest in the public good, but is now quite an activist. The sight of a crumbling Eaglewood Pavilion on the flattened ground is such an eyesore. Dawei clutches his huge head and pulls at the hair … how he wishes he could just sign for his family and move out! Unfortunately, he can't bear imagining others pointing fingers at his back. Words like "surrender" and "chickening out" were taboo to him when he was a little boy playing "Good Cop, Bad Cop." He attributes his sticking around to the influence of the Taoist priest and his own personality.

Soon the rainy season arrives. The chilly autumn rain falls nonstop. The Eaglewood Pavilion looks all the more isolated against the drab background. When night falls, the neighborhood is deserted—the bleakness could almost be interpreted as rustic. However, no resident is in the mood for the poetic. No one finds the patter of raindrops melodious. Instead, it sounds ominous …

Calamity is looming on the horizon.

According to the weather forecast over the radio, Typhoon No. 9 has formed on the ocean thousands of miles away from the Chinese mainland. It will strike Shanghai in three days. The weatherman ends the broadcast by saying, "We'd like to remind all concerned to get prepared." This seems to be specifically meant for the Eaglewood Pavilion. Residents recall that Xiaomao replaced three beams to make furniture. The house is in danger.

People are alarmed. Imagine, on a pitch-dark, stormy night, people are sleeping in their cozy beds. Suddenly, the roof crashes onto them. Doesn't it make your stomach churn? Even Dawei, the calmest of all, can hardly keep calm. On several occasions he is on the verge of warning others against the imminent danger, but he shuts up in the end because he doesn't want to antagonize his neighbors. At dusk one day, an inspiration comes to him as he is lamenting the doomsday. It is some lines of poem he has read somewhere, "... Like the thunderous collapse of a great mansion ... all that's left is emptiness and a great void." These are two lines from different poems in the classic novel *A Dream of Red Mansions*. They're so pertinent that he recites them aloud in spite of himself. As he recites again and again, he gets more and more worked up. Grief and indignation show on his face.

People start to realize there is more to it than meets the eye. They are irritated: Is this malicious joy? What's in it for him if the Eaglewood Pavilion collapses thunderously in the typhoon? Mrs. Huang and Caihua refrain from giving tit for tat, because if the house collapses, it could be anybody's fault but Dawei's!

Dawei's recitation may be unpleasant, but the warning is valid. Residents at the Eaglewood Pavilion set about taking precautions. Mrs. Huang does away with the corrupt custom of demanding dowry from her future daughter-in-law. Instead she delivers Xiaomao's "dowry," as well as their remaining valuables, to the bride-to-be's home. Cynicism aside, Dawei never says no to any neighbor who needs help.

With his help, all necessary precautions are taken, but unexpectedly, the typhoon turns at the Taiwan Strait and heads for the Japanese archipelago instead. People sigh their relief. What a false alarm. The Eaglewood Pavilion is secure for now.

Soon after the typhoon, another alarm is sounded: Mrs. Party Secretary's clandestine deal with the relocation taskforce surfaces! One morning, a four-ton truck pulls up in front of the Eaglewood Pavilion. Several sturdy young fellows get out. Mrs. Party Secretary gives them instructions. In less than half an hour, everything in her room is moved into the truck, and the truck is only half full.

Congratulations seem appropriate, but Dawei doesn't feel like offering it. In fact, anger has been burning slowly inside him for quite some time, and he has lost his usual cheerfulness.

"Goodbye!" Mrs. Party Secretary is enthusiastic.

"Goodbye!" Dawei responds feebly.

Unnerved, Mrs. Party Secretary gets into the cab.

The truck honks its way along the bumpy street. Dawei regrets the "pact" with his neighbors.

Winter descends much earlier than usual this year. Residents at the Eaglewood Pavilion find the house colder than before. According to conventional wisdom, the coldest days are the third and fourth nine-day periods after the winter solstice. However, it is only the second nine-day period when they have to put on warmer clothes. Why? With all houses around them demolished, they've lost protection.

They yearn for fire from heaven, but where is Prometheus? Grandpa Rice Wine has put on his worn, cotton-padded coat. The cloth rope around his waist makes him look like a beggar, if you think the glass is half empty, or like Santa Claus, if you think the glass is half full. Finding time hangs heavy in his hands, he makes pessimistic comments from time to time. When no one pays attention, he resorts to heavier drinking. He now drinks at three meals a day, and each drinking session is longer than the last. Caihua is too agitated to salvage her father-in-law from alcoholism.

Mrs. Huang has had enough sitting at home and waiting for things to happen. She frequents the office of the relocation taskforce to pick fights with people there, hoping that friction can start a spark, and a spark can ignite a big fire ...

The cold war continues. No end is foreseeable. One day, as Dawei sits at home brooding, some well-dressed visitors burst into the Eaglewood Pavilion. He goes out to confront them, but the senior guy in a Mao suit looks quite distinguished. He seems quite familiar with the house, because he is explaining something at length to his young followers—who are dressed in outlandish outfits—as he points to the beams.

Are they here visiting or excavating? They must be mistaken! Dawei's ridicule is almost out of his mouth when the senior guy turns a smiling face to the Taoist priest, who has just arrived home with his head lowered the usual way. Dawei is stupefied, and the Taoist priest is in shock.

"Hey, you!" The senior guy widens his smile as if he were meeting some friend he hadn't seen for years. He grips the hands of the Taoist priest. "Do you remember me?"

The Taoist priest freezes. Yes, I met this guy before, but where? He tries hard to recall.

"I'm Mr. Wei. Don't you remember? You haven't changed a bit! *Kungfu* practice does promote health! Look at me, all kinds of diseases, including cervical vertebra hypertrophy ..." he shakes his head and the bones crack. The Taoist priest keeps blinking.

The Taoist priest feels heat in his palms. How ridiculous it is to allow a stranger to hold your hands! Alarmed, he disentangles his hands, mumbles a greeting, and vanishes into his room.

"Wait!" the senior guy raises his voice. He produces a business card from his breast pocket to present to the Taoist priest. After a slight pause, the latter takes it. He is immediately relieved, "Ah, you, it's you ..."

The handsome gilded printing in Song typeface on the white, scented business card reads: Mr. Wei Sanshi, GM, Shanghai Historic Sites Tourism Development.

Historic sites development? Are they here on a field visit? What a pity they have missed the better days of this ancient building. Doesn't it amount to black humor?

Well, these people didn't intend any black humor. Mr. Wei was the young writer who visited the Eaglewood Pavilion in 1958 to collect folk stories, but this time he has come neither to collect folk stories nor to engage in archaeological studies. He quit writing long ago.

Mr. Wei had since tried his hand at many trades in the interior of China. After retirement, he came back to his hometown of Shanghai, where economic growth was at the top of the agenda. Naturally, he was not to be left out. He racked his brain to find a business where his expertise could be put to use. Finally, he decided to resume his old trade. Shanghai Historic Sites Tourism Development was launched. No enterprise begins without difficulty. There were doubters at the start-up stage. An old friend, who frequented Xinhua Bookstores, told him explicitly: Shanghai isn't even an entry in the newly published *A Dictionary of Historic Cities in China*. If Shanghai is not a historic city, how can you find historic sites here? If there is no historic site, how can you develop tourism on top of it? What can a swallow know of the aims of a swan goose?

He smiled at the friend and immersed himself in work. He had more knowledge of Shanghai than most people. For example, the original meaning of "Shanghai" was actually "going to sea." A dictionary only presents one idiosyncratic view.

After two years, the results were significant. For one thing, he identified the address where Mr. Sun Yat-sen stayed on his first trip to Shanghai. For another, he discovered the former headquarters of the Third Workers' Armed Uprising in Shanghai. His research also revealed the villa of a concubine of Li Huang-Chang, one of the Northern Warlords. He profited from these discoveries by writing brochures, contributing short pieces to newspapers, and showing those houses to anyone, Chinese or foreign, seeking novelty—anything goes as long as it is "historic" and lucrative.

Of course, residents at the Eaglewood Pavilion are in the dark about this. They just regard the uninvited guests with eyes wide open. After some small talk with the Taoist priest, Mr. General Manager turns to whisper into the ear of a Hong Kong person with a round face, long hair, and sunglasses. The long-haired guy nods satisfactorily. Then the two of them pace the passageway twice. The long-haired guy takes off his sunglasses to scrutinize recesses between walls. He even asks the Taoist priest to show his room. He seems to be valuing a long-lost national treasure. People's hearts beat faster: The house is historic, isn't it? Ideas cross their minds. What the visitors do next baffles them. They go out and size up the exterior of the house. Then they walk to and fro on the clearing surrounding it ...

Residents have another idea: Will they dissemble the house and ship the pieces somewhere else? This has happened before. In a foreign movie titled *The Ghost Goes West*, an entire castle was dissembled and shipped to another country, with the ghost in it. Will these people from Hong Kong buy the Eaglewood Pavilion? Otherwise, why do they look so serious and meticulous? But it doesn't seem the case. The long-haired guy starts to gesture as he speaks broken Mandarin. Mr. General Manager is sidelined and gaping ...

What on earth are they here for? Will they shoot a movie here? Probably, because residents detect words like "set" in the substandard Mandarin speech of the long-haired guy. So these gaudily dressed men and women are no dilettante archaeologists seeking excitement out of their usual cafes and dancing floor. No, they are real artists. What's worth special mention is that stout guy with permed hair. He is a red-hot director in Hong Kong.

"Damn! We've got enough trouble. Why don't they go and play somewhere else!"

"Find a garden house to shoot your movie!"

"All these monkey tricks ..."

Residents mumble to each other. They don't want to have one more thing to worry about. On the other hand, these strangers didn't come all this way for nothing. They have given it some serious thought. The clearing around the house is ideal for a movie set. The crumbling house fits the storyline perfectly ... where else can you scout out such a location in the hustle and bustle of Shanghai's crowds? If you don't believe it, try to shoot some scenes at the corner of Nanjing Road and the Bund. Police cordons will be required, and congestion is highly likely.

Trucks deliver square timber and plywood. Workers start to

hammer things together in the clearing. The set is ready in three days—it's a street hailing from the 1930s, with posters reading "Wholesale & Retail" on wire poles, and signs like "Beautiful Brand Soap," "Old Knife Cigarette," "Jewelry," and "Pawnshop" at storefronts. If this were not a deserted area, onlookers might very well pack the set and the Eaglewood Pavilion to the point of collapse.

Kids are having the most fun of it. How they wish to live on a movie set forever! Baobao, who is a first-grader, wants to cut school. Grandpa Rice Wine has to cajole and intimate every morning, "Go to school, kid! The movie won't finish soon. You'll have plenty of time to watch!" Little does Baobao know that his grandpa is lying. The movie people are here for only a few shots. They need to go back to Hong Kong as soon as possible.

Residents at the Eaglewood Pavilion don't know whether to laugh or cry. In the end they are resigned to the fact that a movie is being made right around them. This is a rare experience, though. Most people watch movies without knowing how they are made … it's just that it's not the most ideal time.

Although the scenes and characters in the movie are fictitious, the script is based on a common occurrence in Shanghai before the Liberation in 1949: The landlord wanted to pull down an old house to make room for lane houses; the sub-lessor would like to extort higher rents; tenants had their respective agendas. They maneuvered against each other and their lives were a mixture of tragedy and comedy.

Challenges come one after another as the camera rolls. The director finds he is one leading actor short—the guy who plays the sub-lessor, a role that makes fewer appearances but is essential to the unfolding of the story. As for supporting actors, he planned to tap into the local talent pool—aspiring actors are readily available on the mainland and "art schools" are turning out more.

The long-haired director selects three extras on-site: Caihua, Mrs. Huang, and the Taoist priest. To his surprise, all three raise objections. Take the Taoist priest. He is supposed to play a wandering monk, but he explains to the director that Taoism and Buddhism have always been as incompatible as ice and hot coals. Some Taoist temples have engravings depicting the dark side of monks, whereas in the stone carvings of Buddhist temples, Taoist priests are sinister, sly, bawdy, and sordid ... therefore, he is not about to betray his faith. Moreover, with the White Cloud Temple under restoration, he can't risk losing his priesthood again.

On the other hand, Caihua and Mrs. Huang object because they are shy. Mr. General Manager puts his finger on the crux of the matter. He explains to the two that their work will not be gratuitous. Capitalists in Hong Kong also follow the socialist principle of "to each according to his contribution." The two women are consequently motivated. They barely show their faces in the movie. For example, one of them pours out boiled water from a kettle and announces, "Mr. Hong, you've a visitor!" Another of them lifts a door curtain and smiles obsequiously at the camera. By contrast, Dawei works much harder—he substitutes the Hong Kong actor who was supposed to play the sub-lessor. He has to deliver a monologue of grief and indignation in tears and he shouts himself hoarse. This is a challenging task, because the actor must memorize more than three hundred words and live his part. He must shed tears and choke with grief at the right moments. The long-haired guy proves himself an expert in casting. Dawei may not have the best looks or voice, but he is strong enough to withstand the emotional upheaval of his character—a handsome but effeminate actor might develop hernia!

Dawei is a simple, straightforward guy. If the director thinks so highly of him, he shouldn't be disappointed. Why not have some fun on the side! His wife, Tian Xiaoyuan, regards it more seriously. She understands her husband the best. Big and tall, he is not handsome in the usual sense, but he has the best ethos. Had he not been confined to the culturally desolate Eaglewood

Pavilion, he could have become the Alain Delon of China!

Cameras, flash bulbs, reflectors, musical instruments, everything is in order. The long-haired director, who may seem roguish to average citizens, cries out majestically, "Camera!" Dawei is in the limelight. Here comes Take One ... Dawei blunders. He mixes up lines despite frequent prompting from the script holder. Dawei loses confidence. He starts to doubt whether he has the makings of an actor. His wife remains calm. She helps him see why he failed. He was too eager to live the part and got stuck. Who can blame Dawei? There were so many ways he could identify with his character: The character had gone through a good deal of misery before becoming well-off, yet he was always on the verge of losing his home.

The filming has come to a standstill. The long-haired director decides there is better way to unleash the passion inside Dawei. He tells Dawei to relax, put himself in the shoes of the sub-lessor, and act in a manner he feels comfortable with, as long as it is in line with the plot.

Dawei nods in gratitude for his trust.

"Camera!" Flash bulbs are on again. Dawei paces leisurely into the spotlight in a bowler hat, a Chinese jacket, and trousers. The scene runs as follows: The sub-lessor had been on the go the whole day. He came home looking forward to some rest. But tenants pestered him for repairs, plumbing, and rent cut. At first, he was patient. By and by, he flared up. By this time Dawei has totally gotten inside the character.

" ... Darn! Are you through ... are you really human? Do you have a heart? If you are human, why do you nag all the time, and why do you sneak around hatching evil plots? ... If you have a heart, why do you always put your own gain ahead of anything else ... were your ancestors like you? No, they exhorted the ethical code. You've violated it all with your curses, abuses, and indecency. You're only too anxious for earthquakes, tsunamis, and lightning strikes to happen ... you wish me die sonless. Yes, you're right. I won't have a son to cry at my funeral ... I don't have

son. No. I deserve a son. Where is he? My son, where is he ..."
Dawei breaks down crying.

Ha, Dawei is serious! He was speaking for himself. Ms. Tian
is pregnant! No wonder he has been agitated recently. If it were
not for the movie, where and to whom could he pour out his
woes?

"Cut!" the long-haired director roars. He rushes onto the
set, grabs Dawei's paws, but words fail him. There is a reason
for his excitement: He is a new-school director who stresses
authentic sentiments during improvisation. Afterward he tells
others that Dawei is a memorable extra in his movie career. "He's
gifted." With his disposition and some useful pointers, Dawei can
certainly make an excellent actor.

When Dawei hears about it, he says, "To hell with the gift.
Even a nitwit in my position will lose his temper and come out
with what's on his mind. I was bursting to come out with what's
on my mind ..." He may sound a bit ungrateful, but it was
straight from his heart.

So, is the shooting a complete success? In a way, yes. Dawei's
performance makes the movie more entertaining. Post-production
will handle the slight digress from the script. However, something
else goes wrong and losses are incurred.

According to the schedule, after Dawei's appearance there
is a fire scene. The fire is to be small and containable. As a
precaution, the scene is to be shot on a set—a boudoir built
from plywood. Historic Sites Tourism Development, which
provides package services to the crew, is called on to provide
yet another service: fire safety. Mr. General Manager contacts
the meteorological department and the fire department the next
day. The weather forecast reads: "Southeasterly wind, cat 3 to 4;
wind gust, cat 5."

Sand, buckets, and fire extinguishers are lined up. A match
is struck to set wood shavings on fire. Having made sure that
all risks were ruled out, the director shouts his order, "Camera!"
But somehow the fire is less than satisfactory—it either burns

too brightly for actors to get close or too insipidly to make an impression. Several takes later, the director loses his temper, "... Add more oily cotton waste to the fire. Turn on all electric fans. Miss May, get ready! Action! Shriek fire. On the count of three. Three, two, one ..."

Miss May gathers herself together, dashes into the fire. "Fire!" She draws out the last syllable, creating quite an atmosphere ... good, done. The director goes up to congratulate Miss May. He frowns the moment he takes her hand: What the f--k. She didn't even take off her own diamond ring and her fingernails are painted scarlet. Looking up, he sees jade earrings dangle from her ears. This is totally not how a cobbler's daughter looks!

There is no alternative but to start all over again! Crew members busy themselves cleaning up the set, removing and applying make up, getting into the character, and starting a fire. The director is ready to count down when he catches something out of place: The fire is too close to the sheet! Just then, Miss May appears on his monitor in all her glory. Blame it on his need for a quick success or just habit; either way, the word "Camera!" is shouted out before the director realizes it. Crap! The sheet catches fire! There is a boom and flames fly off in all directions. There is a pause in action. Then all of a sudden, everybody starts to scream and scramble ...

The poor long-haired director stands transfixed. Dawei comes back into the fire to drag him out. On his second trip, he salvages the camera. When he turns to make a third entry, the "boudoir" has been engulfed by fire. After all, the "boudoir" is just some plywood and splints nailed haphazardly together. The strong northwesterly gusts burst open the cracks in its walls easily! With a groan, the boudoir goes down. In a blink of an eye, the fire licks the Eaglewood Pavilion.

It takes a while for everybody, including Dawei and Grandpa Rice Wine, to react. They sprint home and grabs whatever is valuable. In a short while, the ancient Eaglewood Pavilion, instead of ascending onto the list of historic buildings to be preserved, ascends into the sky in the form of smoke …

# IX

People come to visit the debris and meditate on the lessons learned. The culprit is identified—Shanghai Historic Sites Tourism Development.

Some people say Mr. General Manager never contacted the meteorological department or fire department in all his apparent seriousness. Otherwise, why didn't the firefighters come after the fire broke out? Others disagree. They claim to have seen a fire engine race by and a helmeted firefighter hop off it to ask a dumbstruck old man whether all valuables had been salvaged. When confirmation came that all valuables had been removed on the eve of the typhoon strike, he hopped back onto the fire engine. He had hopped on and off in less than half a minute, which was amazing speed. Some people counter that there wasn't any fire engine racing by, while others try to find evidence that there was …

An old man stays out of the discussion. He squats in front of the still smoking debris, clutches his gray-haired head and sobs silently. Who is he? He is Li Rihai, the person who has lived at the Eaglewood Pavilion the longest. Why does the Taoist priest cry? Isn't his son's household registration being processed? Actually, he doesn't care about that all. He has long been disappointed by that ungrateful son. Even since the Public Security Bureau revoked Linglong's household registration, he has pinned his hope on another son, the son that was abducted from his doorstep at the age of five. Although his mother saw a middle-aged woman spirit the child away, the Taoist priest is convinced that this son, who looks exactly like him, just wandered away and will walk in the door on a late spring morning or at dusk on the Moon Festival, addressing him endearingly, "Dad, I'm back!" But now, with the Eaglewood Pavilion gone, how is his son going to find him? This means his son, who should be a respectable adult by now, is forever "lost." How can he not cry?

People sigh and shed tears of sympathy. Dawei comes to realize why the old man was willing to let Caihua and others boss him around. His heart goes out to the Taoist priest, but there is little he can say. For the moment, he has to put his expecting wife before everything.

There is always someone who tries to be wise after the event. Throughout the fire, Grandpa Rice Wine was trembling like an ill-tuned TV screen. Now, the power supply is stable and TV signals are clear. He is telling the story of "Borrowing the East Wind" from *The Three Kingdoms*: Zhuge Liang predicted with miraculous accuracy that there would be east wind in deep winter. As a result he won the bet with Zhou Yu and avoided beheading. As for himself, he heard the weather forecast very clearly: Southeasterly wind, cat 3 to 4. How come God changed his mind and sent northwesterly wind instead? Was this predestination? ... Well, you can't blame Grandpa Rice Wine for such a conjecture, because he hasn't studied dialectics and has no idea of how chance and necessity are related.

Other residents at the Eaglewood Pavilion remain clear-headed despite the mishap. Mrs. Huang warns against superstition and idealism. She believes it was all a conspiracy, "Hmm. This so-called Historic Sites Tourism Development and that Hong Kong director are both traps set up by the Relocation Taskforce."

It hits the mark. Everybody sees light suddenly. It's time to turn sorrow into strength. Yes, the long-hair made us doubt his gender. He looked like a hooligan just released from a correction facility. Right, that so-called General Manager was just a commission merchant. How dare they make us act! They are just clowns ...

"Crap!" Caihua screams and pales. "That guy, the so-called director, I saw him somewhere before!"

"Where? Who is he? Come on!" Mrs. Huang relapses into the commanding tone.

Caihua stumbles around clutching her head as if struck by thunder. It is some time before she shakes off the nightmarish look, "Yes, it's him, the carpenter from the Housing Administration! No wonder ... he looked familiar!"

"Are you sure?"

"I saw him loitering around with a saw on his shoulder."

"I always suspected the camera." Mrs. Huang sounds like an expert, "There wasn't film inside ..." She has a reason for saying so. Although she is not going to mention it, her son once took a date he didn't fancy to the Xijiao Park for a whole day with a film-less camera.

So it was a prank, a trap! They were all duped!

Days later, the former residents of the Eaglewood Pavilion move into the new apartment block along the Huangpu River in accordance with the original plan proposed by the Relocation Taskforce. Once they have settled down in their spacious, bright, and comfortable new homes, they can't but admit that the fire was most opportune.

Dawei believes that the "fire therapy" cures his neighbors of all kinds of dark thinking. One day, when he goes to the local police station to apply for residence registration for his newborn daughter, he runs into Caihua and Mrs. Huang. The conversation he overhears between the police officer and Mrs. Huang stirs up disquieting thoughts in his mind.

"Mrs. Huang, now there is no need to petition for anything any more."

"Yes. This time we are totally, truly liberated!"

"A south-facing apartment with a balcony ... are you happy?"

"Of course. Just that ... forget it. I shouldn't complain. It's much better now!"

Imagine that! A sulky old lady saying she shouldn't complain. Dawei blurts out, "Oh yes. Otherwise someone may end up in prison, not a new home!" He regrets before his voice has died away. He didn't mean to snitch on an old lady in front of a solemn-looking uniformed police officer! ... Feeling Caihua grinding his foot, he adds hurriedly, *"The Law on Relocation* has been promulgated. For those who complain and refuse to be relocated, they'll have a tough time!"

Dawei sounds very sincere.

Mrs. Huang doesn't think Dawei insinuated anything, because in the decades she and Dawei lived under the same roof, they might not always been on friendly terms, but they were by no means nemeses to each other.

# The Loser

One day, Father beckoned to me when he returned from buying his train ticket. "Let's go. Chang Gen agrees to teach you!" I was both surprised and delighted. So Father had Chang Gen's ear!

"Really?" I asked. Father nodded confirmation, told me to change my clothes after lunch and get ready to go with him. I wolfed down lunch but didn't change my clothes. I was wearing a uniform given to me by a relative who had been released from military service decades ago. Mice had left two holes in its sleeves, black cloth lined the collar band, and it was huge enough to fit in two people my size. He had been big while I was still in puberty. I liked this old thing that draped over me because it was "in": The khaki color stood for the vast loessland, the indomitable fighting spirit, and men of valor. Pale and frail, I had no other way to fulfill my fantasy than by wearing it.

The uniform fluttered in the strong autumnal wind. I threw heaps of questions at Father as we marched: How did you come to know Chang Gen? How old is he? How close are you? Will he take me up formally as an apprentice? Can he really regroup broken bones with his bare hands? At that time I only reached Father's shoulders. He straightened his back, and hemmed and hawed tolerantly at my questions.

Actually, I already knew quite a lot about Chang Gen. He was in my personal Hall of Fame. My other heroes included Lei Feng, a PLA soldier who Chairman Mao Zedong praised for his devotion to helping others; Wang Jie, a PLA soldier who sacrificed his life to save a militiaman during a drill (Mao Zedong wrote a dedication to him, which reads, "Fear neither hardship nor death");

Guan Yu, also known as Guan Yunchang, a famous warrior in *Romance of the Three Kingdoms* who was later worshipped as the Saint of War; Qin Shubao, a famous warrior who helped establish the Tang Dynasty (618–907); Dong Cunrui, a PLA soldier who sacrificed his life to blast a Kuomintang bunker; Yang Gensi, a PLA soldier who ignited himself to kill American soldiers during the Korean War; and Bai Yutang, nicknamed Brocaded Mouse, one of the gallants in the novel Three Heroes and Five Gallants, set in the Northern Song Dynasty (960–1127).

Chang Gen lived near our old home, close to my maternal uncle's house; he used to hang out with my father (in a kind of gang, but only for a short while). As a street performer he had performed kungfu by the wharf, which was an urban jungle now but a deserted crematorium back then. He was also very skilled at making energy-efficient stoves—stoves burning egg-shaped or honey-comb briquettes, cupola furnaces, you name it. The kerosene stoves he made with three wicks, six wicks, nine wicks, twelve wicks, and twenty-four wicks used to be the rage of the Old Town. His disciples and followers were all over the world—a relative of mine later took a thirty-six-wick kerosene gasifier, an adaptation of Chang Gen's invention, with him to help the Tanzanians build railways.

The most fascinating things about Chang Gen were his hands. His naprapathy was said to improve blood circulation, eliminate stasis and swelling, set broken bones and tendons, and cure old wounds. If he chopped the air, water in a basin would splash out, leaving a mere drop or two behind. As a result, patients came in swarms; trucks, cars, wheelbarrows, and tricycles packed his street. Thank God there were no parking meters yet. From those vehicles, able-bodied companions carried out groaning, emaciated patients. His house was Medina to them and he was Jesus Christ. Pilgrims came from all walks of life, from senior officials to longshoremen, farmers, fishermen, and peddlers. They lined up outside his door and coexisted peacefully. Everyone was at the beck and call of that magic pair of hands.

Father passed those myths to me, which he had heard at the teahouse when he came back to Shanghai to visit us, so much so that the name was worked into a song in my subconscious:

Chang Gen has a pair of magic hands,
magic hands,
that cure all diseases,
all diseases,
hernia, epilepsy,
and it's all for free,
for free ...

I was a frail child. My parents spent much of their income on my hospital visits. What with Father's stories and the nondescript song in my head, I was drawn to Chang Gen and wished very much to see this legendary figure in person. Now Father was taking me to pay a formal visit to him and he was going to teach me something. How could I not fall into a reverie?

I was anxious that a master of his caliber might not want to share his life-saving skills with me. The reason I pestered Father with questions on how close they were was because I feared cold-shoulder treatment or worse—downright rejection. According to some book I read, the best and the brightest distinguish themselves from the crowd either by extraordinary looks, such as earlobes touching shoulders; or an unusual voice, such as a sonorous one; or odd behaviors, such as feeling for lice in front of authority figure, or rolling their eyes at every turn. In short, history has proven that it's difficult to meet a big shot, let alone get close to him.

Father led me past our former home—my maternal uncle and his two good-for-nothing sons were still living there—and across three lanes, where we reached a black door with peeling paint. This *shikumen* house looked no different from its neighbors. Father attacked the big round knocker in a familiar way. The knocker hit the wooden door with a blunt noise. I backed off instinctively. Something might leap out from behind the door. Father's large bulk would be the best shield. After a while, the headstone-like black door creaked open. A round, fleshy, reddish face popped out. At the sight of us, the sleepy eyes widened, and a cheer erupted. "Wow, it's you!" With that the door was thrown wide open. A short old man materialized in front of us. Pointing at me, Father explained to him in our native dialect: This is my son. I bring him along for what we have agreed upon. He nodded and sized me up. Then he showed us in.

So this was the famous Master Chang Gen. Although he was amiable and not at all condescending, I couldn't but feel disappointed. Was it him? How could it be him? His looks—a short rotund figure, a meaty chin and two slitted eyes—were a far cry from the heroic image in my imagination. I preferred an awe-inspiring and mean master to such a benevolent little old man. The latter was unreliable, in my opinion.

After we took our seats, Father struck up a conversation with Chang Gen, apologizing for disrupting his afternoon nap, inquiring about his "business" and chatting about miscellaneous topics unrelated to me. Chang Gen yawned constantly behind his meaty palms, the subject of wide speculation. He then made responses as if he were at a press conference. They both spoke our native dialect. The atmosphere in this small room of roughly ten square meters felt cozy, and I grew drowsy.

We were in his living room. It was cramped and barely furnished. What caught one's eye was a small plank bed in the center of the room. It was similar to a hospital bed, but much shorter. I commented to myself that maybe wonders were always made in cramped environments. Many accomplished people succeeded despite adversity. Similarly, many celebrities were born with physical flaws. Physical flaws might discourage some people from pursuing success, but they might also encourage others to try harder.

Since we'd interrupted Chang Gen's afternoon nap, Father felt it appropriate to take leave as soon as possible. I plucked up my courage and bid him farewell solemnly. Father said, "My vacation will be over soon. I'm leaving Shanghai tomorrow. Please keep an eye on my son."

Master Chang Gen smiled noncommittally. Father produced a bag of unprocessed tubers of multiflower knotweed he had collected in his spare time. The herb was said to have made General Yang Ye (a gallant warrior in the Northern Song Dynasty) almost immortal. Chang Gen accepted it with both hands before promising to take care of me. I had the impression that he didn't actually want me as an apprentice. This was quite typical of us Chinese: With Father in a similar trade to his (Father was a medical doctor), he would lose face if he agreed too readily to take me on. Nevertheless, I had to praise Father's acumen in gift giving when I caught glimpses of Master Chang's gray hair on the temples. I had read from a scrap of paper inside an empty bottle that the indications for tubers of multiflower knotweed included juvenile hoary hair, geromorphism, and fatigue. So this was the right gift for Master Chang Gen at the right time. Moreover, it didn't cost much.

That being said, when I grew up and learned more about traditional Chinese medicine, I knew how wrong both Father and I had been at that time. Only processed tubers of multiflower knotweed were effective in reversing hoary hair, while raw (unprocessed) ones might cause diarrhea. I wondered if Master Chang Gen ever took the raw ones we presented him with. If yes, all would be well if he happened to have constipation, but otherwise, too bad.

It was settled that I should come to study at 8 a.m. Mondays, Wednesdays, and Fridays, when Master Chang opened for "business."

Once home, I sought Xiaomei out to tell her about Master Chang. Xiaomei was our neighbor across the lane. She was not impressed, since her father was a medical doctor too, although he had been out of a job for years.

The next morning, after having some cooked rice soaked

in boiling water for breakfast, I changed into my old uniform and made efforts to look smart. I strode confidently on my way to "acquiring some skills." But the cookie-cutter houses in Master Chang's neighborhood were simply confusing. As I stood hesitating, I noticed people walk toward a black door in twos and threes. It rang a bell. My eldest cousin had told me that Master Chang's house was crowded with people and vehicles. This must be the right black door.

Was I late, or were others early? The living room was already packed. There were people sitting or standing in the courtyard, which also served as kitchen. I elbowed my way through disgruntled people until I reached Master Chang. He was already sweating. I stood there timidly, unable to make the simplest announcement that I had arrived. Finally, Master Chang looked up from the shoulders of a patient. When our eyes met, I blurted out, "Uncle Chang." I assumed that "Uncle" sounded more endearing than "Master." His palms kept working the shoulders. His huge head slumped twice like a sunflower. Sensitive as I was, I immediately realized my mistake. A master is master. "Master" was not to be mixed up with "Uncle." I blushed. But the humiliation was soon overcome when I saw the eagerness in the patients' eyes. I felt taller. It was great basking in my master's glory.

Master Chang Gen's session with the patient was over without my being aware of it. He called out to someone behind me in a husky voice, "Ah-Fa!" A pair of strong arms shoved me. I gave way meekly but my eyes were vicious. This guy was taller than I by a head and older by a dozen years. He had bushy eyebrows, large eyes, and a thick bronze torso. Days later, I learned that he was Master Chang's senior apprentice, a "barefoot doctor" (a term created in the 1960s, referring to part-time paramedical workers who serve rural people) at a factory.

The senior apprentice stood respectfully in front of Master Chang, ready to take orders.

Master Chang winked at him knowingly. What happened

next made my heart quail.

A short, middle-aged man was pinned to the wooden bed face down. The senior apprentice took off his sneakers, leapt onto the bed, and stood between the patient's legs. Master Chang peeled off the almost-new Mao suit. Underneath it was a starched white cotton shirt with cloth buttons down the front and slanted pockets, something I had only seen in movies. He rolled up his sleeves, bared his muscular arms and squatted by the bed. Next, he put his right palm on the patient's small of back, his left palm on his own right arm, and uttered one word: "Up!" The senior apprentice grabbed the man's thin ankles. Just as he lifted them up like a cork, Master Chang pressed down with a "ha!" Something seemed to crack. What followed was a choreographed pas de deux, with the senior apprentice shaking the patient's feet in step with Master Chang's hand movement up the waist and to the chest. The room was filled with an energetic work song of "Ha! Up! Ha! Up!" while the tiny male patient writhed like a rattlesnake. The three of them presented to the onlookers a simple, primitive, but graceful dance …

At the end of the dance, all three were perspiring profusely. The tiny man sighed one sigh of relief after another. The senior apprentice preened. Master Chang was gasping like an ox that willingly bore the burden of hard work.

I was stunned. Afterward, when I asked another apprentice, who had been initiated a little earlier than I, what the "dance" was for, he cast me a contemptuous glance. "Ischialgia!" I nodded and tried hard to memorize it.

The first session made my heart quail. The second session had my heart all aflutter.

The senior apprentice, who had shoved me into a corner of the room, ordered me to fetch a cold towel. Running errands was expected of any apprentice. I was only too eager to oblige. I pushed my way through the crowd, pulled a towel off a rack in the courtyard, and doubled back. As Master Chang reached for the towel, he beckoned me to stand closer. I supposed he wanted me to observe as well as listen to his instructions.

Gratitude welled up inside me.

The next patient in line didn't look ill at all. A young married woman in her thirties, she had a good complexion, raven-black hair and dark eyes, a full figure and an expressive face. Apparently it was not her first visit, because she had tucked her bob behind her ears, and removed her coat and sweater before Master Chang opened his mouth. I stepped back to allow her more room. Now she was in a thin, tight-fitting undergarment with a lotus embroidered tantalizingly across her boobs. She lay on her belly without being told. My eyes took in her well-shaped legs. Hm, the senior apprentice had a problem. It was always a delicate issue handling female patients. A man couldn't just grab their legs and shake at will, right? It would be satisfying to see the senior apprentice, who had spurned me a while ago, appear coy and get scolded by Master Chang.

To my disappointment, the senior apprentice didn't get onto the bed. I edged closer, ready to "steal" some secrets of the trade like those I had read in books.

Master Chang washed and dried his hands, lowered his stout trunk laboriously, bent his fingers into an impractical orchid's shape, and lifted the young woman's undergarment with two fingers. Something glared. It was her white, smooth, naked back. My heart skipped a beat, my cheeks flushed, and I felt as if I were standing on clouds. I seemed to have drifted into a small, warm, dark room in a thick down vest, where numerous jade-like naked backs swirled. They zoomed in and out of my vision until the back of a huge torso froze in front of me. I saw one unfathomable well after another. Inside the wells I saw clear, rippling water out of which rose rows of swaying tender scallions. I soared into the sky and looked down. Below me was vast, snow-covered farmland crisscrossed with footpaths. All of a sudden, I plummeted to the ground as if someone had pulled the flying carpet from under my feet. I opened my eyes. Master Chang was still in a squatting stance. Lips tightened, he ran his thick palms up and down the naked back in an unhurried manner. There was no sign of discomfiture.

I loathed my own frailty. But then a line by Lu Xun came across my mind: True warriors dare to face bleak life. The pale thing in front of me should be part of life. If I didn't dare to look at it, how could I acquire skills?!

I forced myself to look at it. Unfortunately, the moment I did so, all kinds of weird thoughts came to me. It was too much. Without knowing it, I made my way through the attentive spectators, out of the house, into a public toilet, and peed into a urinal briefly.

I fell in love with the place, the atmosphere and the arousing spectacles.

Master Chang held me in awe. He was a towering deity in my mind. Yes, his looks were plain, he didn't have lofty ideas, and he spoke with a heavy accent, but weren't deities always appearing in the vile skin-bags of mortals, anyway?

Some new, vital force was swelling inside me and fighting to get out. It made me restless. A vent must be found.

One day, I wandered into the Nine-Room Building across the lane without knocking at the door. Xiaomei was in bed in her clothes. Embarrassed, I was poised to leave. But doing so would make my behavior even more dubious. So I took a seat by her bed, instead. This was a cramped room. There was only a narrow aisle between two beds. Rumor had it that her family used to be rich—of course, back then they didn't live here, and they had come down in the world since the onset of her father's illness. According to Ah-Ming, Xiaomei's father had mental disorder, which was quite credible, judging by the latter's maniac conduct. However, since I had seen with my own eyes how Ah-Ming went out of his mind, there was always a risk accepting his claim at face value. Something hit me: Why didn't I check Xiaomei out before? Now I really, really wanted to.

Xiaomei was lying on her side on top of some folded quilts. The top button of her shirt had been loosened. I could catch a glimpse of the soft bulge underneath her ivory neck. Her surprisingly full figure was in sharp contrast with her thin, sallow face. A pale blue vein stood out on her left cheek. There were dark circles under her eyes. The shirt of red patterns on white ground was a bit too tight. She wasn't pretty, yet her body ... my eyes fell on the lower hem of the shirt, which happened to be slightly awry ... I caught myself arranging my fingers into a clumsy orchid's shape. My palms were wet. My heartbeat was arrested.

"What!" Xiaomei's eyes widened all of a sudden. There was a glint of shrewdness.

I hemmed and hawed. Then it all came back to me. I had come to tell her about Master Chang Gen. So I plucked up my courage and described what I had experienced with him in recent days. Of course I kept my mouth shut as to those feelings that might invite rebuke from her. Xiaomei was uninterested. I said: Wasn't your father in the same trade? Why the scorn? She sprang to her feet and shoved me out.

In the past two weeks, Master Chang had opened my eyes.

He seemed to see patients indiscriminately, be they suffering from heart diseases, nephroptosis, nocturia, or thyromegaly. His specialties spanned multiple departments in a conventional hospital: traumatology, orthopedics, internal medicine, gynecology, and pediatrics. Moreover, he neither prescribed Chinese herbal medicine, which was the rage of the age, nor endorsed acupuncture. He simply relied on his hands, the beefy hands of moderate size that had become legendary among his believers.

Take heart diseases for example (like polycardia or arrhythmia). He just drew his fingers together, spread his palm on the patient's chest, arched it and let it fall several times. It was said to be more effective than some well-established drugs like Practolol or Digitalis.

Many women who worked at textile mills suffered from

nephroptosis, a chronic occupational disease resulting from standing on one's feet for too long. The more severe cases called for a surgery to secure the kidney with surgical catgut. A likely complication was infertility. The daughter of one of Master Chang's friends got nephroptosis owing to stringent control of her waistline. She sought Master Chang out after many other failed therapies. In a few sessions she was able to avoid surgery. News travelled by word of mouth. Slim-waisted girls started to visit in swarms ...

There was another pretty girl with nocturia. Despite her smart outfit, light figure, and nice features, she was on tenterhooks every night. Living with other girls in a dorm or out-of-town travel was out of the question. One day, her mother took her to see Master Chang. The girl flushed in embarrassment when she had to discuss her symptoms within the hearing of so many strangers. Master Chang understood. He agreed to treat her last. As noon approached and all but one patient had left, the mother and daughter grew all the tenser. The senior apprentice was in no hurry to leave, but I had to. The next day, when I reached Master Chang's house, the senior apprentice was asking him how to treat nocturia. Apparently, Master Chang or someone else had sent him away. Pointing at his own pubis, Master Chang was about to enlighten his studious disciple. But I went in, and he shut up. The senior apprentice was not pleased.

Events like this spiced up my life immensely.

The pity was Master Chang was not a very enthusiastic teacher. The senior apprentice was an ass-kisser, but no more favors were bestowed upon him except for such physical exertion as shaking patients' legs. Master Chang had already had a lot of well-established pupils. His second apprentice was in military service, and his fourth pupil was president of a hospital. Fatigue arose with regard to younger pupils, naturally.

Sometimes, I felt aggrieved, but in all fairness, who did I think I was? Had my father not had any knowledge about herb gathering or former association with Master Chang, would

Master Chang have taken me in, a frail teenager? Such thoughts drove me to study in my spare time the few dilapidated medical books my father had left behind. They were on meridian points, the four diagnostic methods of traditional Chinese medicine (looking, listening, questioning, and feeling the pulse), herbs, metals, and stones. However, as I studied, my mind frequently went off into wild flights of fancy: On one hand, I was eager to become someone like Master Chang; on the other hand, the tedious stuff in books was far less interesting than fantasizing how Master Chang's meaty palms moved under a woman's panties or on her breasts. Of course, from time to time my thoughts were more sober: How did he manage to make a heart beat regularly, and how did he restore those elliptical kidneys to where they belonged?

I was so obsessed that I dreamed about trying my hand at therapies ...

A month and a half had passed. Master Chang was still cool towards me. Sometimes he even made me sit on a stool against the wall to keep out of his way. Later, under his instruction, I succeeded a self-taught doctor from a factory as his "bonded house slave"—I swept, washed vegetables and rice, and cooked. The only thing I was exempted from was washing baby diapers. Poor me. Having seldom gotten my hands dirty at home, I was now a male maid at Master Chang's ... I did bemoan my fate and my father's insipid relationship with Master Chang, but at the same time I reminded myself of the inevitability of the seniority system and how Yang Shi, a Song Dynasty (960–1279) scholar, stood in the snow to wait on his master, Cheng Yi.

I kept a close eye on Master Chang, looking for a break.

Master Chang's temper swung from kindness to foulness in an unpredictable manner, which made even the senior apprentice, a superb observer, feel at a loss. He was obsequious to most patients, accommodating their sometimes-unreasonable demands. Yet for the rest of patients, his service was perfunctory.

As patients came and went, some "VIPs" emerged. Not only did they enjoy higher-quality treatment, but Master Chang also went to great lengths to make their lives easier, which was touching.

An old man and a couple of young married women were the VIPs among all VIPs. The former was partially paralyzed. Whenever his mumbles were heard, Master Chang would push through the crowd, greet him smilingly, and help him gingerly into the room.

"How are you doing, Uncle Zhang?" Having settled the old man into the already-vacated bed, Master Chang beamed at him.

"Fine. I'm much better now, Dr. Chang." The old man broke into an innocent smile.

"Lift your arm for me!" Master Chang was in high spirits. He stepped back, squinting his long, narrow eyes, as if expecting some miracle: The old man raised his stick of an arm above his chest and then his head.

Half of his face shivering, the old man tried so hard that he drooled. The withered arm never went higher than the third button from his neck down.

"Try again. Come on!" Master Chang was patient.

"Last, last night, I raised, raised it to my, my throat . . ."

The old man laughed at himself shyly. His efforts didn't pay off. The arm went back drooping. "I know something is wrong since this morning. Gosh!" Relapse was understandable. Master Chang encouraged him, "Take things easy. It happens. I'll work extra hard for you!"

Master Chang focused on his hands. He was soon out of breath and sweat oozed out of his forehead. Meanwhile, the old man sang praise of Dr. Chang to onlookers despite the difficulty of speech: Having been paralyzed in bed for more than two years and dismissed by fifteen hospitals, he had finally found his savior. "Yes, Dr. Chang. My savior!" he chanted in conclusion. Others echoed.

Master Chang toweled off cheerfully. The old man denounced his unfilial son who insisted on sending him to another hospital.

He'd rather die than submit. He had no faith in the Goddess of Mercy or Jesus Christ, but he trusted Dr. Chang. As a proof, he fumbled out a brown medicine bottle from his pocket, with which his son intended to poison him. "Look. That scoundrel makes me take poison!" He passed the bottle to Master Chang, who immediately changed his countenance from mercy to disapproval.

With one look at the bottle, Master Chang shook his head slightly and sounded hurt, "Uncle Zhang, didn't I ... tell you ... that if you come to see me, you can't ... they cancel each other out. I ..."

Before he could finish, Uncle Zhang had smashed the bottle onto the cement floor with his good left hand. "What do I need this damned thing for?"

The old man's face reddened all over in happiness. Master Chang smiled magnanimously, "Easy there. You can't afford to lose temper!" He gave the old man an endearing pat on the back. "Have more patience!" Uncle Zhang laughed like a naughty child. Master Chang called out, "Ah-Fa, take Uncle Zhang home!" Thereupon the senior apprentice borrowed a three-wheeler to send the old man home, while I swept the broken glass from the floor.

Several days later, at the sound of Uncle Zhang, Master Chang left other patients to help him in, and the same ritual was performed again.

As the time passed, I found Master Chang's confidence in his therapies approached superstition. He seemed to doubt any other art of healing, especially Western medicine. He refused to treat anyone who was taking Western medicine or injection behind his back, however hard the person implored with teary eyes. His logic was simple: If you believe in him, why would you take Western medicine? Faith is key to positive outcome. Without it, how do you expect to recover? Therefore, what he needed in a sense were not patients, but disciples who trusted him religiously. This might sound narrow-minded, yet not over-the-top to a self-assured medical professional.

Unfortunately, neither the senior apprentice nor the other elder apprentices had caught the subtlety.

When "business" wound up that day, the senior apprentice made a gaffe in the courtyard when he found that the little pills mingled with broken glass in the dustpan were actually made from gastrodia elata. "Wow, they're gastrodia elata pills! Aren't gastrodia elata plus rutin compound the right protocol for paralysis?"

Master Chang, who was taking a rest on a square stool, responded coldly, "What do you mean? If gastrodia elata and what-do-you-call routine are so effective, why are there still people paralyzed or suffering from cephalemia? Alas, you ... try them with pigs tomorrow, will you? Gastrodia elata, what the hell ..." He sighed heavily. His disappointment was audible.

The senior apprentice was disconcerted.

I had a vague sense that Master Chang was not too pleased with us apprentices. See, even the senior apprentice, his right-hand man, could be a wet blanket. That was because we were not devout believers in him and his skills. No wonder he told the senior apprentice to feed gastrodia elata to the pigs, and ordered me about like a servant.

Days of observation had made me realize how seriously Master Chang took his teaching job. He had always insisted on the absolute authority of a teacher. He cold-shouldered me when I reported for duty the first day, because I addressed him as "Uncle Chang." Later, I was clueless enough to address him as "Master Chang" instead of "Master." He didn't respond at all. Even later, I became a little wiser and followed the example of elder apprentices. I lowered my head deferentially and used my sincerest voice. "Master!" Then and only then did he respond in his husky voice. I could sense his content and pleasure.

The senior apprentice had a special way to address Master Chang that cheered the latter up. Listen to him. He finished the word "Master" with a slight drawl, something that you could give infinite interpretation of. As a routine, Master Chang was warmer in his response.

"What is it, Ah-Fa?" Apparently he liked the drawl. The pity was I was unable to imitate. Neither did I dare. What if my poor imitation made me a laughingstock? Anyway, the senior apprentice had exclusive claim over the drawl.

Master Chang really believed in the saying that goes, "One day your teacher, all life your father." Since we were all sons to our fathers, we simply had to treat him in the way we treated our fathers at home. For example, you should not interrupt him or elder apprentices when they talked, you should not crack jokes at him or elder apprentices, however wise you considered yourself, you should not walk ahead of him or elder apprentices, you should stand still and sit straight, you should not lie to him or elder apprentices, etc. Anyway, Master Chang might be an easy-going, kind old man, but he was not a slipshod teacher.

Consequently, when Master Chang asked after my father or wanted my opinion on my father's medical skill, I always answered frankly and sincerely. "Father hasn't written recently." "Father wrote me the other day. He sent his regards." "Father only knows how to dig up herbs. He is not as capable as Master!" "Father urges me to be humble and take every opportunity to learn from you!"

My ready answers triggered Master Chang's smile and the following comments to the elder apprentices, "His father used to be my junior fellow apprentice. Well, he is being polite. Your father is a very capable man!" Then he grew thoughtful. "Remember, perseverance will prevail!"

My ears burned at his words. Who did he think lacked perseverance? Was it my father, me, or the senior apprentice? His advice, together with the sigh, was weighty and unsettling.

To be frank, I would have quit a long time before if my father hadn't urged me repeatedly in his letters to learn from

Master Chang and not to lose face. Once, having had enough of Master Chang's overelaborate formalities, I wrote a lengthy letter to my father complaining about it and pointing out how humiliating it was for him to have his son's status reduced to that of a servant.

Ten days later, a registered letter from my father arrived. In it, not only did he rebut my argument, but he also praised Master Chang lavishly, including his efforts to improve himself despite childhood diversity, his fine character, and his superb medical skills. He ended the letter by writing, "Seize the opportunity and learn from Master Chang, or I won't see you again!"

He had underlined the sentence so hard that he ripped the paper. There were also three bold exclamatory marks!

Even if I didn't fully appreciate the letter, the tubers of multiflower knotweed he had presented to Master Chang stopped me from giving up halfway. Little did I expect the favorable turn this letter would generate for me.

At the end of business hours one day, as I was making the bed, Master Chang, who was sipping tea leisurely on a square stool, asked me out of blue, "Has your father written?"

"Yes." I stood taller. "It's registered mail. It's all about you!"

"Me? Like what?" Master Chang arched his brows.

I let go of the sheet, threw out my chest, and gave a quite accurate account of what was in the letter from memory. Master Chang cut in before I could finish. Radiant, he gestured, "Show me next time!"

Why not? Master Chang was illiterate, anyway.

I agreed readily. Little did I anticipate the consequences. In due time, I presented the pile of letter paper my father had scrawled over to Master Chang, who had presumably forgotten about our conversation. It took him only a second to realize what it was. He took it with both hands. I thought he would squint at it in the sun making like he was reading it and pass it back. To my surprise, he handed it to the senior apprentice, who had just gotten in, beckoning, "Read it out!"

He sat against the wall like the Maitreya Buddha, palms folded over his abdomen and eyes narrowed into slits. By that time, patients started to arrive. Ah-Fa, the senior apprentice, cast me a meaningful glance before reading out the letter in a louder-than-usual baritone, "Sancai my son!"

Sancai was my infant name. Thanks to his cadenced recitation, now everybody knew. Patients regarded me with surprise. How I wished I could sink through the ground. Why had I revealed the content of my father's letter to please Master Chang, and why had I given this humiliating letter to him when he had almost forgotten?

The only relief came from Master Chang, who sat with drooped eyelids and swung his head slightly throughout the process as if enjoying a nice pot of tea. The senior apprentice had come to the three bold exclamatory marks. Master Chang waved him stop before he could read out my father's instruction for my mother in the next paragraph. I was ready for Master Chang to fetch the letter, with the senior apprentice's spit on it, and return it to me. To my surprise, he sat up contentedly, looked around the staring patients serenely, folded the letter, and locked it into his mysterious medicine cabinet.

I had no idea how Master Chang justified such an act—he never returned the letter. He couldn't go as far as to keep it as a kind of evidence, could he?

When I left Master Chang that day, he asked me solemnly to come back in the afternoon and help him make herbal preparations. An apprentice who had been initiated slightly earlier than me told me on our way home, "Now it's official. The Master has taken you in!" What? I thought I had been his apprentice since day one.

He dismissed my protest by pointing out that the Master only asked real apprentices to help him in the afternoons.

"That is to say, I wasn't ..."

"Right."

Gosh. After attending him for two months, Master Chang

didn't even consider me a real apprentice!

My nose caught something intoxicating when I first entered Master Chang's crowded treatment room, something similar to the pervasive smell at a brewer's. I had speculated whether it came from armpits or Master's Chang's mouth, but the senior apprentice seemed the most suspicious. I knew very well one mustn't drink during "consulting" hours. As the old maxim goes, "When the wine is in, the wit is out." Just look at Xiaomei's father. He was drunk all day long, loitering around, shooting off his mouth, and behaving in an obscene manner. Just imagine how, with the touch of a doctor, the wine molecules infiltrate the skin, vessels, nerves, and even bone marrow of a patient and wreak havoc. When it comes to the doctor under the influence, it would be hard not to be tempted by patients' nudity.

Master Chang had good work ethics. He never touched a drop of wine.

Then, from where did the strong aroma emanate? Investigations led me to a small wooden cabinet converted from a niche for a statue of the Buddha. It was known as the medicine cabinet. There were two shelves inside. On the top shelf were five or six used saline solution bottles. On the bottom shelf was a pile of toilet paper. In the bottles were reddish brownish roots or tubers steeped in liquor, the Chinese home recipes known as medicinal liquor, the source of the aroma.

Those of us in the know called the medicinal liquor the "dressing." After Master Chang's massage, a patient's body (or back, belly, arms, legs), like a drought-stricken prairie, was in dire need of a good rain. As soon as a liquor bottle was unplugged, the aroma got into one's head. Two or three sheets of rough toilet paper (never the fine tissue people use nowadays) were spread out, and the medicinal liquor was sprinkled on them. The wet toilet paper was then applied to the skin that was still warm from rubbing. When the skin dried off, a fresh deck of wet toilet paper was applied. The number of applications depended on the severity and duration of the disease.

Since such folk therapies were said to be quite effective, the demand for medicinal liquor was huge. Five or six bottles could barely last us through a week. The production process was elaborate—it took at least a fortnight for ingredients to age in top-quality Qibao Liquor. Master Chang rotated about twenty used saline solution bottles.

The recipe was naturally top secret. All recipes were guarded jealously and passed on from one hand-picked successor to another. Master Chang used discretion. As a rule, he divided the work among few trustworthy apprentices on the afternoons following his morning "business hours."

No favorite apprentice got the entire picture. Each apprentice was sent out to purchase one or two ingredients. It was Master Chang who mixed all ingredients and bottled the final solution.

On that day, either it was because of my father's letter, or it was a momentary oversight, Master Chang disclosed the entire recipe to me: six onions, two hundred and fifty grams of ginger, twenty-five grams of fennel, twenty-five grams of clove, fifty grams of mastic, several wilted roots of Chinese chives ...

As I tried to commit the recipe to memory, I could hardly contain the shock. How was it that such common ingredients in the average kitchen work wonders? It was ingenious for Master Chang to come up with another use for them. Master Chang summoned me back to reality, "Your father mentioned some sort of 'threadrum.' Can you write it down for me?"

"..." What? Was it silk thread, thread for shoe soles, or thread for the sewing machine? I was clueless. However, catching the cold glint in Master Chang's eyes, I thought this must be some sort of pass-or-fail test. I almost confessed that Father had never mentioned the word to me. I glanced at the senior apprentice timidly. There was mockery in his eyes, but at the same time he was thoughtful. Anxiety seized me. Too bad my father had told Master Chang what a big fan of traditional Chinese medicine I was. Too bad I had been acting as if I really knew about TCM. Now they would all know the sham I was.

"'Threadrum.' Your father said it kills the pain and relieves rheumatism ..."

Could it be as asarum? I blurted the name out. "Yes, yes, yes!" Master Chang was excited. He passed me a sheet of toilet paper. Without hesitation I wrote down two large Chinese characters standing for "asarum" with a pencil. I was secretly pleased with myself. The credit went not to Father, but to my own study. As I put the pencil down, I caught the envy and admiration in the eyes of the senior apprentice.

Master Chang sent the senior apprentice out for asarum immediately.

I hoped that it would strengthen the curative effect of the "dressing."

It took me a long time to win the good opinion of Master Chang, but a very short time for me to bow out!

Having spent time with Master Chang for more than two months, I got the sense that Mrs. Chang, whom I had never met, was not very enthusiastic about her husband's enterprise, and that Master Chang was a bit henpecked. Whenever Mrs. Chang had the day off from work or was on a sick leave, Master Chang hung out a sign that read "Away," and shut the door. Patients with appointments had to reschedule.

I had never witnessed Mrs. Chang's reign of terror, but according to an older apprentice, you didn't want to experience it. How bad could it be? He shuddered and turned pale. Keeping this in mind, I went meticulously about the tasks Master Chang assigned to me: I washed vegetables leaf by leaf until they glittered; I ran the rice under the tap and picked out every little impure particle; I swept the floor; I wiped all the furniture, including the shabby reclining chair in the courtyard, at the end of each morning we were in business. In short, I didn't want any sloppiness on my part to provoke grievance in Master Chang's eldest daughter, who commuted daily from another district to have lunch at her parents', or his two other daughters who were still in the middle school. Mrs. Chang would see to it very soon and Master Chang would suffer.

Sometimes I thought it was unwise of Mrs. Chang to frown upon Master Chang's "sideline," for it was quite lucrative. Of course Master Chang never accepted cash. I still remember a nursery rhyme that all street kids seemed to sing around that time:

Who will take my three-wheeler?
I will.
What's fare?
Serve the people, free is only fair!

As you see, the trend at the time was to "serve the people," and Master Chang could hardly go against it. Moreover, primitive communism seemed to have desensitized people to money. That being said, patients felt apologetic to Master Chang, who had sweated over them. They brought him farm produce as a sign of gratitude. Master Chang always declined. But then they insisted. So he deferred in the end—it was unreasonable to ask them to carry such heavy items all the way home. Even better, he could give some gifts away as tonics—Master Chang had the firm belief in "you are what you eat." He gave pork kidneys to slim-waisted girls, pork trotters to paralyzed patients, and pork hearts to cardiac patients.

Therefore, I thought Mrs. Chang knew too little of the ways of the world. Thanks to Master Chang, her family had more food than they could eat, food that was a considerable portion of an average family's budget. Wasn't it nice? Well, a thing is valued in proportion to its rarity. Mrs. Chang must have seen such gifts too much to care (the average household at that time didn't possess a refrigerator). I was worried about Master Chang's enterprise, and I didn't look forward to meeting Mrs. Chang.

However, I was to meet her very soon.

One day, as I was cleaning up after the last patient had

departed, a pair of plump feet strutted into my sight. I looked up. It was a well-dressed woman with upward-slanting eyes. I soon realized this was mistress of the house when she asked coldly, "Is the rice cooking?" I gripped the broomstick harder and swept with extra vigor, hoping very much to make amends for Master Chang's fault.

Although I dared not watch her, Master Chang's soft voice reached my ears, "Why are you home so early?"

"I asked for sick leave!" her tone was steely. Master Chang introduced me to her. She broke out into a smile and started a string of pleasantries such as "put the broom down" and "it's so kind of you." Then a well-anointed delicate hand took the broom from me. Closer up, her brows were two thin plucked lines and her small chin was tucked in.

"How is your father? Has he written recently?" she was still smiling.

Surprise, she knew my father! I warmed up to her. She offered me tea. Master Chang beamed. He would be all right. I declined and took leave. Mrs. Chang would not listen. She wanted me to stay for dinner. I'd better not yield. The ping-pong game of politeness went on until the black gate creaked open and a lively face popped up. Without knowing it, I had cast Master Chang a glance. His face immediately darkened. The gate opened wider and framed a voluptuous young married woman who chirped, "Dr. Chang, sorry I'm late!" My mind went blank before recognizing her. She was the heart patient to whom Master Chang had passed on many chicken intestine, gizzards, and hearts. Master Chang looked quickly at his poker-face wife. He appeared tense and embarrassed. Just then, Mrs. Chang banged a rice bowl onto the table.

"I, I," Master Chang stuttered, his accent was thicker than usual, "my blood pressure went, went up ... next, next time ..." The young woman took the cue. Her eyes swept over everyone. With a sweet "goodbye" she was gone.

In my opinion, fresh produce alone should be reason enough

for Mrs. Chang to support her husband's enterprise. There must be something more fundamental. But young as I was, how could I tell?

Soon afterwards, Master Chang closed his business. He didn't explain why. My short apprenticeship was over. I went back to loafing around: keeping goldfish and playing audience to Ah-Ming.

If Ah-Ming had not been sick, he would have married already. He wanted to have sex so badly that he was able to direct any conversation toward that topic. People categorized him as an anthomaniac by convention (the other two categories being raving maniacs and armed maniacs). In my knowledge, however, he flipped out not because of his sexual obsession, but because he made some wrong remarks at the wrong time to the wrong people. Therefore, I didn't regard him as a true anthomaniac, my evidence being that he never referred to sex when he was taken ill and that he could talk about nothing else but sex as soon as he was restored to reason. He had a bag of tricks to move the flow of conversation seamlessly towards sex, ranging from catching at shadow and innuendo to explicit language.

Ah-Ming's opener was often Xiaomei's father. To him, the latter was the really sick person, although some people thought he feigned madness while others believed that he was simply keeping a low profile. As a result, he made reckless comments about Xiaomei's father. Coincidentally, Xiaomei's father preferred being treated as sick, since then he could shoot off his mouth and put on obscene acts whenever he felt like like it. Not only did he not take offense at Ah-Ming, but also he sometimes wrapped an arm around Ah-Ming's slender neck and called him "bro."

Xiaomei hated her father's guts. Whenever she found her father in Ah-Ming's company, she raised her voice and ordered him to go home.

For her sake, I didn't hang out with Ah-Ming a lot. Xiaomei had other objections to him. Sometimes when I dropped in on her, she craned her neck to check the surroundings. When we talked, she cast frequent fleeting glances at her window, which opened onto the hallway and showed every passer-by. At first, I thought she was fascinated with people watching. Only later did I find out that she was on the lookout for Ah-Ming.

According to her, Ah-Ming often crouched near the window to eavesdrop, which was at once disgusting and scary.

Xiaomei seemed to have a crush on me. She received me pleasantly even if she knew I had just parted company with Ah-Ming. Her job assignment still pending, she had a lot of time on her hands. Therefore, she cleaned and decorated her home meticulously. It was refreshing to sit inside her simple but elegant room after an earful of Ah-Ming's graphic ravings. However, such a refreshing experience didn't come easily. Callers were only allowed in fixed time slots: In the morning, if you intruded before she had finished cleaning, you'd be shooed out; in the evening, once her father was home, she greeted any uninvited guest with the clatter of utensils; after lunch, she didn't mind visitors, but you wouldn't want to deprive her of her daily siesta.

Her figure filled out gradually, thanks to the daily nap. But her face grew sallower and her spirits drooped, which was quite puzzling.

One day, after lunch, with nothing better to do, I headed for the house across from mine again, only to find Xiaomei had latched her door for the nap. Ah-Ming materialized just in time. He smiled at me enigmatically. "You're thinking about it, aren't you?"

"About what?" I was baffled.

He made an obscene gesture. I flushed and spat at him.

Unoffended, he stated matter-of-factly, "Stop fussing. All men think about it! Unless you are not a man!"

The categorical assertion held me in awe. Although I had never given it any specific thought, sexuality lurked in the back of my mind. He seemed to imply that I was not "not a man." With a pat on my shoulder, Ah-Ming enlightened me: It was normal to think about it and abnormal not to. A normal man, especially a man who drinks, needs sex in order not to disrupt public security.

Speaking of a man who drinks, Xiaomei's father came up in our conversation, naturally. According to Ah-Ming, Xiaomei's father had told him that he needed sex every day. "Don't you wonder about Xiaomei's mother?" Her mother did look ill and listless, but what did that have to do with sex? Ah-Ming gesticulated as he babbled on. There was admiration in his eyes. "He showed me. He was awesome! That day, he … " I was too embarrassed to hear more, but he interpreted my embarrassment as distrust. As a result, he insisted that I verify it with my own eyes the same night.

That night, I had barely fallen asleep when someone called out my name outside the house. Damn, it was Ah-Ming. He was serious. I went out to stop him before my family grew suspicious.

Ah-Ming's eyes glistened on his solemn face in the faint streetlight. He pouted his lips at me, "It has started. You're just in time for this …"

Heart thumping, I followed him in spite of myself. Whether it was out of curiosity or fear, I couldn't tell. We arrived at the hallway. I backed away, but Ah-Ming's bony hand gripped me. "Don't you chicken out. Now look into the window. Check out the double bed facing you. Do you see anything?" His mouth stank.

I pushed him away instinctively, but my eyes went involuntarily toward the window. As they got used to the darkness inside, I made out the faint outline of the furniture, and then of something white undulating in bed …

"Have you seen it yet?" Ah-Ming whispered enthusiastically. "Look … have a good look at it!"

To tell the truth, I was unable to make head or tail of it. A long sigh from the other side of the wall killed my question to him. Then, someone turned in the bed. Xiaomei must be still awake. I almost cried out. Ah-Ming was too engrossed to notice my slipping away.

At noon the next day, I went to probe if Xiaomei had

found out about us. As I hovered outside her door, Xiaomei happened to come out. My face reddened abruptly. She was warmer than usual. Not only did she invite me in, but she also talked in high spirits. However, sleepiness soon descended on her. She yawned several times, begged my pardon, and lay down in her clothes.

My life was as dull as ditchwater.

My elder cousin alleviated my boredom with constant visits and news about Master Chang: Chang Gen is back to work. Chang Gen started making stoves again. Chang Gen caught a meter-long eel in the Huangpu River ... The news was so depressing that I drew a mental picture of a dejected and downtrodden Master Chang. Things turn into their opposites when they reach the extreme. After a month or so, Master Chang's luck turned for the better. Soon afterward, my younger cousin reported one exciting piece of news after another: Chang Gen is seeing patients again. Chang Gen cured a patient who had been paralyzed for five years. Chang Gen was driven away in a car to treat a VIP ... Well, then I drew another mental picture of Master Chang, one in which he stood tall and heroic.

The news was so encouraging that I went back to the familiar alley with fear as well as anticipation, like a longtime traveller returning home. As expected, Master Chang's business was returned to its former glory. The small room was packed. So was the courtyard. Some patients even stood outside the gate like sentinels.

To my delight, Master Chang's business had more than recovered. A screen was now protected the privacy of the patient undergoing therapy, and each patient was holding a bamboo chip with a number on it. In the meantime, to my sadness, some younger apprentices out of nowhere had usurped my position, which hadn't come easy. The senior apprentice bossed people around like a commander-in-chief. Master Chang appeared to be busier than ever, so busy that he ignored me.

I stood desolately in a corner. Nobody paid me any attention. How I missed the kind Mrs. Chang.

At dusk one day in late autumn, as I stared at the setting sun feeling abandoned by the entire world, a potbelly preceded Master Chang into my home. "Master!" I called out excitedly. What an honor! He nodded at me graciously. I offered to make tea, but he waved a hand, the hand that so many people worshipped, at me.

"No, next time. We have a patient to visit!"

"We?"

"Of course!"

Gratified that Master Chang sought me out, I put down the teacup and asked him where the patient was. I had to inform my mother, otherwise she would raise hell and hunt me down.

"Not far from here. A friend referred a neighbor of yours to me!"

"What's wrong with the patient?"

"Headache!"

I was filled with deep esteem for Master Chang, who was willing to visit a patient suffering from such a minor discomfort as headache, despite his busy schedule.

We chatted as we strolled. Not having to compete for Master Chang's attention against those ass-kissing elder apprentices, I tossed at him all kinds of questions I had been burning to ask: Is it true that if he chopped the air, water in a basin would splash out, leaving a mere drop or two behind? Could he really sleep on three upright chopsticks? ... He just smiled. When I pressed further, he hemmed and hawed absent-mindedly: Those rumors confuse him with his senior fellow apprentice. I was skeptical. Was he being modest? On second thought, if his senior fellow apprentice was so capable, surely he was good too. On the other hand, my senior fellow apprentice was no good at all—he was just an apple polisher.

Without knowing it, we had made several turns, crossed several roads, and reached a compound. In the twilight it looked as gloomy and cluttered as a war zone.

We walked on a narrow path. Master Chang stopped in front of a red-lacquered door on which a round mirror hung. He coughed, and the mirror quivered. He knocked. After a long pause, a skinny man wearing a broad smile greeted Master Chang softly, "Hello! Here you are, both of you. Thank you so much … I've just put her to sleep!" He was very apologetic.

"Who is it?" a weak voice inquired from inside.

"Shoot," the man shrugged in desperation, as if he were a kid exposed in a game of hide-and-seek. "See, neuroticism. She hears everything …" He then turned around, "Here is Dr. Chang!"

A hum of acknowledgment was followed by tiny moans.

There was a weird smell in the darkened room. It might be the mixture of toilet water and herbal medicine. I pinched my nose to get rid of the irritation. Master Chang greeted the patient in bed, but I could make out nothing. The man clicked a light switch. I expected to see a room flooded with light, but only a three-watt lamp was turned on. The dim greenish light was just a drop in the bucket of the spacious room. Chill crept up from my toes.

I came to realize that Master Chang was talking about my father. Did they know my father? I was stunned. Then Master Chang started to sing high praise of my intelligence and diligence. When he finished, he cleared his throat loudly and his voice boomed, "Come on, show us what your father has taught you!" What did my father teach me? Nothing! The reason I knew "asarum" was because your indifference to me had stimulated me to study on my own! "Come, come over. Take her pulse for a start!" Master Chang sounded so confident in and proud of his prodigy disciple.

This was embarrassing. I sweated and my heart pumped so hard that it might burst at any time.

"Come with me." The man, whose curiosity was apparently aroused, steered me toward a wide bed; my soul seemed to have detached itself from my body and hovered in midair to observe my body being seated on a square stool by the bed. However, what remained of my consciousness kept reminding me: Don't let Master Chang down. Don't make Master Chang look like a fool. I decided to go ahead at any cost.

I half closed my eyes. A soft, white, fleshy hand was put into mine. My earlobes grew hot and twitched. My mind went blank. Luckily some lines from Li Shizhen's *Diagnosis by Feeling the Pulse* hit me and I didn't lay my fingers on the hard ulna, which would be telltale enough. A sudden electric current jolted me. Maybe I was shaking, or we both were. But somehow I couldn't feel the pulse. Was it my panic or the fat of her hand that blocked the signal? Or had I just lost the tactile sense? Sweat dripped into my eyes and made them burn. I pressed with force, only to feel the chubby wrist again. I had made a fool of myself as well as Master Chang. I was not a prodigy. Neither was my father a medical doctor. How I hoped that Master Chang could come to my rescue, but he didn't know anything about feeling the pulse!

Having my back to the wall, I calmed down. My fingers felt some slight stir, like a signal transmitted from beyond our universe. There it went again, around *cun, guan, chi*, the three places at the wrist where the pulse was supposed to be taken … I glared and clenched my teeth, determined to catch the signal. Tut, tut, tut. Was it my heartbeat or her pulse? I had no idea. I closed my eyes and fell into a trance. I was trudging through a deathly marsh, not knowing what was ahead. The wind howled. Snowflakes drifted. A wisp of smoke rose in the vast desert far away. The wind carried the wail of a woman. It had been too long. A small bonfire was built in the wilderness. I played with a match, curled up in a pitch-dark cave. The cold matchstick seemed to have grown feet of it own. Grip it. Don't let it go. It spit out a red flame. My fingers were hurt …

The minute felt as long as a century. Unable to hold back, Master Chang coughed. He was warning me: It has been too long. Now say something! I woke up, felt the pulse closely, and, with a reddening face and plucked-up courage, declared to the expectant audience, "Thready, rapid pulse!"

To tell the truth, I had no idea what "thready" and "rapid" meant.

Master Chang hummed encouragingly. "Now check the coating on her tongue!"

A bright fluorescent lamp was turned on at his instruction. I instinctively raised a palm to shield my eyes. It was also a good opportunity to wipe the sweat off my forehead. A white handkerchief came into view. It was wrapped around the top of a pale face. Below it was a young, elegant face. My vision blurred, and my senses went blunt. There was no way for me to check the so-called "seedling of heart" inside her mouth.

Master Chang coughed softly. Feeling his eyes fixed on my face, I blurted out, "The tongue coating was thin and yellow!"

"Good!" Master Chang approved at the top of his lungs. He nodded at the master of the house, who was sizing me up in surprise, took his seat in an old-fashioned rosewood armchair, raised a white teacup, sipped loudly, and spit out some yellow phlegm with force.

The sun died out in a blink. I fell into a hell of glittering will-o'-the-wisps, where my soul was purged of its sin. What a relief.

Master Chang made further inquiries about the patient's condition before promising to deliver a prescription in two days. We rose to take leave. On our way back, I asked Master Chang what his diagnosis was and how the woman was related to the man. Master Chang declined to answer except for a curt "headache." Feeling snubbed, I shut up. Still, I was worried about the so-called "headache." According to that dilapidated traditional Chinese medical book, which was often suspected as porn, there were at least seventy-two types of headache, such as migraine, general headache, headache due to pathogenic wind-heat, headache due to pathogenic wind-cold, gripping headache, and throbbing headache. Which type of headache was the woman suffering from? I couldn't help but ask Master Chang. Moving his heavy trunk at a leisurely pace, Master Chang seemed to be lost in thought. After a long while he spoke slowly, "It will take a simultaneous attack from within and without to cure her headache. I'll see to the attack from without, and you'll be in charge of the attack from within."

I was dumbfounded. What was the attack from within and how was I supposed to get started? Master Chang ignored my questions and ordered me to look it up in my father's medical books.

I deeply regretted showing off a moment before.

Knowing Master Chang, I had to get started. Once home, I holed up in the attic and pored over moldy medical books. Still, I didn't have a clue. One afternoon, I fell asleep over the books and had a weird dream. When I woke up, an idea struck me. I was like a blind man trying to size up an elephant. Without undertaking the four methods of diagnosis and checking the eight principal syndromes, how could I come up with the right diagnosis and treatment?

At dusk, I made up my mind to make a house call on my own. This being my first "solo flight," I was both nervous and excited. Before setting out, I dropped in on Xiaomei to brag. She sneered and said something discouraging. I was demoralized, though there was still some fight left in me.

Mustering my courage, I knocked at the red-lacquered door. The round mirror on it shivered and glistened. Was anybody in? I knocked harder, only to be startled by how loud it was. Nobody answered the door. As I turned to leave, the door was unlatched. It was the man, face pale and hair rumpled. He recognized me. After a brief display of shock he pulled me in hastily and locked the door behind us. Only then did I realize he was in his underwear.

I felt guilty about interrupting their afternoon nap. On second thought, no I didn't, because it was already dusk. I explained hesitantly why I was back. He didn't hear me out. Instead, he disappeared hurriedly into the dark inner chamber.

Soon I heard the thump of flesh against some hard surface. Sobs followed. I had no idea what had just happened inside. After some rustling, the man, now wearing his pants, invited me in. The sobs became more audible. They were interspersed with whispered curses. The man fussed over the woman, comforting her in a low voice, so much so that he almost forgot my presence. Only after the woman calmed down did he look up at me with an embarrassed smile. As the fluorescent light went on I saw he had tears in his eyes. The woman's young, pretty face was exposed in the bright light once again: Tears glistened at the corners of her eyes; slightly curled, dark hair framed a wide, pale forehead. With a tired smile she parted her red lips obediently. I had a good look: The tongue was dark red and the coating was thick and yellow! There was not enough courage left in me to feel her pulse. Casting a final look at the unforgettable face, I told the man to turn off the light.

The man saw me off to the door. He grabbed my hand and tears fell like rain, "Thank you, and it is so kind of your master. Please help us." He dabbed his eyes with the front of his sleeveless shirt.

I dragged myself home thinking about the man who looked much older than the seriously ill woman. My mother, who had gone to Xiaomei's home three times to see if I was there, was not too happy with my dejected look. I had to let the cat out of the bag. She cut me off sternly, "I'll not allow a second time! Who do you think you are? What if you kill her?"

From then on, she set herself against my studying under Master Chang. She was a woman of foresight. The young woman, who was twenty years her husband's junior, died before our prescription was delivered.

She died of brain cancer. It was none of the seventy-two types of headache.

Father sent an oral message for me to keep studying under Master Chang. According to him, when all other trades languished,

Master Chang's wouldn't. He even predicted that Master Chang's business would flourish.

Things went contrary to his wishes. I couldn't study under Master Chang anymore. For one thing, my mother objected. For another, physical strength was a must in this trade. One had better have arms as strong as the senior apprentice's and practice kungfu since a very young age like Master Chang. I knew nothing about kungfu. My thin arms could hardly become muscular overnight. Besides, Master Chang didn't tailor his instruction to my aptitude.

Again at loose ends, I raised pets at home: In addition to goldfish, I also raised crickets. Sometimes I went chitchatting at Xiaomei's.

Before long, Xiaomei was assigned a job. Somehow she started to cold-shoulder me. When I braced myself and called on her to talk about her factory, she was standoffish. She was emaciated, and her sallow face had darkened. According to Ah-Ming, she had fallen out with her father. She insisted on living in the factory dorm, while her father wouldn't allow his only child to go away. She declared that she hated him and all other men on earth. Then she cried her heart out hugging her mother, whose figure was wearing to the bones. Her father, who had always been cheeky, sighed and groaned. Afterward, she moved into a dorm and never came back, even on holidays.

The dull life became duller.

Fortunately, my school summoned us "back to school as a way to carry out revolution." Thus preoccupied with "revolution," I pushed Master Chang and his hands to the back of my mind. Later, we were sent to work in factories or rural areas. I didn't have time to revisit Master Chang. Only when my classmates discussed in high spirits the good, brave fellows and their nicknames in *Heroes of the Marshes*, about which I knew nothing, did I miss Master Chang and his admirable hands. Sometimes, not wanting to be ignored, I exploited any tiny opening in my classmates' animated discussion and guided their attention to kungfu and anything associated with kungfu. It was only a matter of time before I dropped the name of my master, Chang Gen.

On most occasions, this trump card worked. Some people, awed by my capable master, regarded me with certain respect. However, in certain cases, a classmate would cut me off, roll his eyes at my frail body, sneer, and resume his comments on Zhang Fei (a key general during the Three Kingdoms Period) and Li Yuanba (son of Li Yuan—the first emperor of the Tang Dynasty), as if implying: What bullshit! Is your master on par with Li Yuanba, the number one warrior under the sun?

For this reason, I missed Master Chang. However, I felt ashamed to go back to him, because I had taken French leave and deserted him when he most needed me.

I was and still am grateful to Master Chang. Although he didn't impart magic skills to me, my unusual association with him adds color to my otherwise lackluster life. It even smoothed my way in dating girls.

In fact, it was Master Chang who helped me maintain a three-month relationship with a girl I had a crush on during the year I took up my first job.

Shortly after we had met, I wanted to hold her hands. She forbade it. We argued. She didn't want to see me again. Master Chang crossed my nervous mind. If I had Master Chang's hands, surely she would put hers into them? I switched our conversation to my first master—Master Chang. Time had eroded some memories of him, but other memories stood out. The latter were all about his hands. On that day, I was so carried away that I created a god out of Chang Gen by mixing his deeds with folklore and fairytales. She was deeply impressed and looked at me with new eyes. She asked if she could see Master Chang. By no means would I allow her to expose herself in front of so many onlookers. But then I found out it was not her, but her mother, who suffered from rheumatoid arthritis and needed to see him. I was relieved.

That would be an easy appointment—just massaging her joints with the "dressing."

I said no problem.

Afterward, I found myself in a pickle. I had lost contact with Master Chang. Neither had I heard about him from my cousins. How was he faring? Would he acknowledge me, a dropout?

After work one day, I made a special trip to my uncle's. My younger cousin, a devout fan of Master Chang's, was not in. My older cousin was drinking alone. A dish of fried peanuts was in front of him on an upturned water vat. He invited me to drink with him. I declined, saying I had to visit Master Chang later. He chortled. After mocking my relationship with Master Chang, he looked pleased with himself and advised me to stay away from Master Chang's theatrics.

Theatrics? Surely Master Chang meant business?

"It is theatrics." Arching his short, thick brows, my elder cousin made a funny face, "His reputation has been ruined!" I asked why. He just urged me to drink. After half a cup of wine, he smacked his lips and sighed, "Well, Chang Gen's happy time is over." Had he drunk too much? No, maybe he was right. Xiaomei's father, a properly trained medical doctor, had resumed practice. With him and his colleagues back in the market, where could Master Chang go? I felt sorry for Master Chang, for his poor, lonely old life in "a deserted house with few callers."

"What on earth happened?" I insisted on getting to the bottom of the matter.

Sipping at his wine with gusto, my elder cousin just evaded my question. When pressed, he breathed alcohol into my face and challenged, "What does he have to do with you?"

Speechless, I was not willing to let the matter go. There should be proper closure: Back then, Master Chang created wonders with his hands and won huge crowds of followers. Yet, due to lack of adequate preparation psychologically, mentally, theoretically, and materially, he ended up being "completely routed." As a one-time disciple of his, shouldn't I draw from this historical lesson? On second thought, such closure was nonsense, too.

I didn't visit Master Chang. My girlfriend of three months broke up with me—Master Chang was no longer seeing patients and she had no cause to visit him on her own.

According to the traditional code of conduct, it was my obligation to visit Master Chang and comfort the man who had fallen into obscurity, but I didn't want the sight of me to stir up his recollection of the glorious past. In the end, I didn't visit him.

Things don't always go as we wish. I didn't want to face Master Chang, but I ran into him unexpectedly. Xiaomei cold-shouldered me, but she married me owing to some chance factor.

Two years later, the old houses in our neighborhood were earmarked for redevelopment. We had to move across the Huangpu River to live in Pudong. I missed my old home, former neighbors, and the alleys where I grew up. When all was quiet at night and I looked out of the window at lights blinking from residential complexes in the distance, a feeling of infinite sadness would overcome me. Alas, how time flew, how human life was full of turns and twists, and how youth had slipped away. Scurrying around in this world, I had forgotten my ambition to master traditional Chinese medicine!

My father had retired. His passion for herbs was replaced by a passion for gardening. Seemingly, he was determined to become the Tao Yuanming—a hermit poet in the East Jin Dynasty (317–420)—of modern times.

Once, he fell sullen over the death of some overpriced, exotic flowers. I suggested that he grow medicinal herbs, since they were cost-efficient, easy to keep, and their fragrance was good for health.

He liked my idea. His old passion was revived. He started to grow lowly achyranthes aspera in fancy flowerpots. He experimented with making bonsai out of astragalus roots, and grafted prunella spikes onto tea trees in the hope of harvesting flowers and seeds to make a refreshing tea that could suppress the hyperactive liver and calm endogenous wind. He even planned to crossbreed Chinese yam and sweet potato with a goal of developing a new cash crop that was good as both food and medicine. For the last project, he wrote to the Academy of Agricultural Science for help, outlining its adoption nationwide and naming it after my niece—Diana I.

Driven by ambition, my father followed the path of Li Shizhen, a pioneering pharmacologist in the Ming Dynasty: He went wherever there were interesting herbs and dug them despite extreme weather. Imagination didn't become an old man. Disaster was looming—one day, upon returning home from an herb-gathering hike fifteen kilometers away, he fell down with a distorted face.

He was partially paralyzed, a blow old people feared the most.

When relatives and friends visited him, they made quite a few suggestions. One relative arranged for my father to get treated at a major hospital, but the outcome was just so-so. My younger cousin recommended Master Chang, who was still seeing patients. Suddenly reminded of this one-time master of mine, I offered at once to get Master Chang from Puxi the next day. My father gasped for breath—which meant he objected. What? Was he unwilling to be treated by Master Chang? Didn't he believe in Master Chang?! I was displeased. If my father hadn't had faith in Master Chang, why did he make me his apprentice? Wasn't it a kind of misspent youth? In the end, my mother suggested our former neighbor, Xiaomei's father, who was an acupuncture specialist at a major hospital. My father didn't utter a sound. He acquiesced.

The next morning, I got up very early with a view of finding Xiaomei's father before he left for work.

Striding along the uneven cobblestone road and looking at the familiar buildings of my youth, I grew emotional. The buildings and the alleys were the same as they had always been, but there were now farmers selling their produce to passers-by with baskets. The one novelty was a grayish stone two meters square on the open space in front of the Nine-Room Building. I remembered a newspaper story a while ago: In celebration of Xu Guangxi's 350th birthday, the municipal government held a ceremony to place an engraved stone in front of his former residence. The stone did add a sense of solemnity to the ancient structure.

A few people were scattered around the stone. I approached the stone out of curiosity. I wanted to find out what the red characters on it said. However, before I was able to do so I saw the face of a familiar stranger. Master Chang! Chang Gen!!

What was he doing here?

Master Chang looked different. He was aged, his tangled, dry, gray hair draping tiredly over his huge head. His face was bigger than before. Whether it was due to obesity or bloating, I couldn't tell. Upon a closer look at his flabby face, I found gum in the folds of his eyes.

Master Chang sat on a low wooden stool, his heavy body leaning against the foundation of the stone, and his hairline on a level with the engraving that read "Former residence of Xu Guangxi, the Ming Dynasty." A piece of white fabric two-*chi* (approximately 66 centimeters) square was spread on the ground in front of him. On it were smeared characters that vaguely resembled "massage" and *qigong*. He was talking as he put one hand on the shoulder of an old lady and massaged her arm with another, but his voice was too husky for me to hear clearly. He could be talking about this ancient building.

I was stunned as well as amused: stunned because Master Chang had come down in the world, amused because he had shrewdly positioned himself in front of a building erected three or four hundred years ago in order to advertise himself. The ancient building and ancient medical skills seemed to endorse each other.

Nevertheless, Master Chang was not a true-blue businessman. His techniques were so elaborate that one motion might last three to five minutes. He also talked as he worked, to relieve his customer's anxiety, anger, or boredom. I was unable to make out his motive. Was it a way to ensure service quality, win more customers, or entertain himself?

I felt an urge to step forward and say hello, but seeing how focused he was on his patient, I refrained. Moreover, I couldn't afford to greet him, let alone reveal the reason why I was here—seeking the help of a medical doctor living in the Nine-Room Building. If he knew a professionally trained medical doctor resided here, he would be too embarrassed to parade his skills. I didn't have the heart to deprive the old man of the one thing that made him get up and out every day.

Without him noticing, I stepped quickly into the ancient but graceful building. Xiaomei's father had left for work. Her mother was still thin as a stick, but with rosier cheeks. She had retired a long time ago. The small room was spotless. I inquired about Xiaomei and her work. According to the old lady, Xiaomei, like before, didn't live with them—but she and her father were on much better terms now. She was studying at an evening college. When I asked about her husband, the old lady looked displeased. Apparently I had touched a sour spot. Xiaomei was still single. I quickly stated the aim of my visit. Without hesitation, she promised to send her husband over.

She said her husband's hospital had just allocated a new apartment in Pudong to them. The keys would be ready in a fortnight. "We'll be neighbors again. It's very convenient!"

My father recovered gradually. Because of our fathers, Xiaomei and I grew closer. However, never did I imagine that my encounter with Master Chang that day would be my last.

It was my cousins who brought the news of his death.

According to my cousins:

Master Chang spent his last days by the stone in front of the Nine-Room Building across the street from our former house. He ran a brisk "business" by accosting passers-by, housewives who shopped for fresh produce, and pensioners patronizing the nearby teahouse. Averaging five to eight customers a day, he made some money, but not much. The problem was, with advancing age, his hands were not as strong as before and his therapies were not entirely satisfactory. Besides, it was awkward for patients to undress themselves in a public venue.

As a result, he adjusted service items. In addition to the "five lesions of heart, liver, spleen, lungs and kidneys in traditional Chinese medicine" and "seven injuries"—a concept in traditional Chinese medicine referring to injuries caused to the spleen by overeating, to the liver by rage, to the kidneys by lifting heavy weights and sitting too long on wet ground, to the lungs by wearing too little and taking cold food and drinks, to the heart by sorrow and anxiety, to the body by abrupt weather changes, and to the consciousness by immoderate fear—internal medicine, gynecology, and pediatrics, he also treated difficult miscellaneous diseases that big hospitals considered headaches or embarrassments.

Speaking of the difficult, miscellaneous diseases, they were indeed difficult and varied, such as the odd thirst for cold drinks in winter but hot noodle soup in summer, no sneezes whatsoever for over three years, and compulsive head shaking upon smelling perfume. More often than not, those people who sought his help suffered unmentionable diseases: male reproductive dysfunction, female physiological dysfunction ... to them, Master Chang was so kind and benevolent that they could pour their hearts out. Sometimes, when business was slack and he needed companionship, he answered questions in great detail without missing the subtleties, as long as the question was asked sincerely. His answers contained knowledge from books, life experiences, and anecdotes.

Such a way of knowledge dissemination had its merits and demerits. On the plus side, it improved listeners' understanding of science, dispelled superstition, solved problems for people and alleviated their suffering, promoted matrimonial harmony, turned lovers into married couples, and helped people realize their dreams. The downside was that indiscreet people might take advantage of him and ask obscene questions.

One high noon, as Master Chang was leaning against the stone lazily, two young men approached him. One was tall while the other was short. One was fair-skinned while the other was darker. The darker one had sprained his back. Master Chang received him gladly. He charged only 50 cents for half an hour's serious massage. To top it off, he shared many practical life experiences, for free.

The two young men's interest was aroused. The darker guy offered his wrist and asked Master Chang to give him a thorough checkup. Master Chang laid the wrist on his knee, closed his eyes and pondered (which I doubted, because he didn't know how to feel the pulse). After a long while, he told the darker guy: He had adequate kidney water, exuberant vital essence, and good appetite. He could live to eighty-nine years of age if he watched his diet. Illiterate scoundrels that they were, the two young men looked baffled.

Master Chang had to explain in plain language: If a person has a good appetite, he eats heartily. The darker guy nodded, saying his appetite was "quite good." Master Chang went on: If a person has exuberant vital essence, the vital capacity of his lungs is huge, and he won't be short of breath after a long-distance race or mountain climbing. The darker guy again agreed. He was a long-distance champion, able to hold his breath in a basin of water for four minutes when he was eight, and swim eight meters without taking a breath. However, he had difficulty understanding "adequate kidney water." Master Chang explained patiently that kidneys were the source of virility. Still, the darker guy didn't get it. Master Chang had to further elaborate: If one has adequate kidney water, his kidneys function extremely well. In simple terms, he is easily aroused and his wife is satisfied; in more exact terms, their sexual intercourse lasts longer; in more explicit terms, his wife gets pregnant readily (therefore they must take caution and use protection). When he finished, the darker guy scratched his head and sang high praise of the diagnosis.

The fairer-skinned guy couldn't wait to offer his wrist. It didn't take Master Chang long to make a diagnosis. His conditions were in sharp contrast with those of the darker guy: He was weak and his kidneys, which were so vital to male adults, were extremely deficient. Needless to say, this was serious. From now on he had to give priority to "the conservation of kidney essence" in his diet and daily life. Master Chang gave him three "commandments": sexual continence, abstaining from desserts, and taking seven grains of coarse salt every morning. The darker guy roared with laughter. The fairer guy's face reddened.

"But I don't understand. The kidney deficiency you spoke of ... I don't think I have it!" Master Chang cut him short coldly, "You'll change your mind if you check your sperms with a 'miniscope.' If you don't believe me ... go ahead and have your sperms counted. See if their numbers are above average or below, and if there are deformities ..." The fairer guy shut up. He had never had his sperms counted. Moreover, he didn't understand how they could be counted!

Master Chang was confident. The two men patted him on the back and complimented, "What clairvoyance! We're convinced!" They paid him ten yuan each (approximately 2 US dollars).

However, a month later, the fairer guy came to Master Chang begging for help. He was worried, because he had got a woman who was not his wife pregnant.

"But I thought you were married, aren't you?" He was married, but he had an affair with another woman—after being told by Master Chang that his sperms were no good.

"Please, use your magic and help me out ..."

"What ..." Master Chang was at a loss for words.

This was tough. This was a life-and-death matter. Master Chang had enough sense left to say no. The fairer guy made a scene and threatened to sue him as an instigator. If Master Chang didn't want to meet the police, he could pay two hundred yuan (approximately 44 US dollars) to him instead. Master Chang went ashen and shivered all over, not knowing what to do.

Master Chang holed up at home to stay clear of the scoundrel. He was angered, worried, scared, and grieved at the same time. Economic loss and summons from the court loomed above him. A week later, when he got up in the morning to brush his teeth, his head hit the tap and he never came back to life …

The above version was provided by my younger cousin, who was a fan of Master Chang and a Chinese major at a TV university.

His elder brother, my other cousin who was still single on the verge of forty, offered a less dramatic version of Master Chang's death. A younger, stronger man who sold quack medicine had usurped the place in front of the Nine-Room Building. Master Chang moved his business to a park. Returning home from the park one day, he died from cerebral hemorrhage. My elder cousin had no interest in literature. His rendering was free of embellishment.

I was confused. My elder cousin had always scorned Master Chang, but his story was fair and sounded true. On the other hand, did my younger cousin, who had admired Master Chang, make a clown out of Master Chang to show off his literary attainment?

I was unable to decide whose version was true. Anyway, Master Chang ended his once-glorious life with a tragedy. As a one-time student, I was grieved for a long time. Since the news of his death reached me too late, I didn't attend his funeral. This memoir is a way to pay my final respects to him.

Excursus: I asked my father, who was still in rehabilitation, for comments on this memoir. He said I had been relatively faithful in my depiction of Master Chang, but I should have given a more in-depth discussion of his abilities. My father also said, given Master Chang's early glories, the part on his being blackmailed by racketeers should be removed. Also, Master Chang died a natural death, not from stroke.

My father also instructed me to delete anything related to Xiaomei. For one thing, I had created something out of nothing. Secondly, I had digressed from the theme. Thirdly, Xiaomei and I were engaged. Our marriage would be the happy ending readers expected.

I will give serious thoughts to his comments. I will definitely leave Xiaomei out of the story.

## Stories by Contemporary Writers from Shanghai

A Nest of Nine Boxes
Jin Yucheng

A Pair of Jade Frogs
Ye Xin

Ah, Blue Bird
Lu Xing'er

Beautiful Days
Teng Xiaolan

Between Confidantes
Chen Danyan

Breathing
Sun Ganlu

Calling Back the Spirit of the Dead
Peng Ruigao

Dissipation
Tang Ying

Folk Song
Li Xiao

Forty Roses
Sun Yong

Game Point
Xiao Bai

Gone with the River Mist
Yao Emei

Goodby, Xu Hu!
Zhao Changtian

His One and Only
Wang Xiaoyu

Labyrinth of the Past
Zhang Yiwei

Memory and Oblivion
Wang Zhousheng

No Sail on the Western Sea
Ma Yuan

Normal People
Shen Shanzeng

Paradise on Earth
Zhu Lin

Platinum Passport
Zhu Xiaolin

River under the Eaves
Yin Huifen

She She
Zou Zou

The Confession of a Bear
Sun Wei

The Eaglewood Pavilion
Ruan Haibiao

The Elephant
Chen Cun

The Little Restaurant
Wang Anyi

The Messenger's Letter
Sun Ganlu

The Most Beautiful Face in the World
Xue Shu

There Is No If
Su De

Vicissitudes of Life
Wang Xiaoying

When a Baby Is Born
Cheng Naishan

White Michelia
Pan Xiangli